EVIL ON THE FRONTIER

EVIL ON THE FRONTIER

by

PETER E. S. KING

Stethoscope Publishing

105/2 Clarke St, Crows Nest, NSW 2065 Australia

First published in 2025 by Stethoscope Publishing

Text © Peter E. S. King
Cover artworks by Ted Lewis
Design by BKA+D

Typeset in Adobe Garamont Pro

Printed and bound by Ingram Spark

978-1-7638987-1-4 (paperback)
978-1-7638987-2-1(eBook)

Evil on the Frontier, King, Peter E. S.

A catalogue record for this book is available from the National Library of Australia

Dedicated to my friends

Barry Rowland Walker
Coolabah Policeman 1983-1985
Retired in Dubbo as Sergeant in 2003

and

Darren Koenig
Dubbo policeman 1987-2012

THIS IS BOOK TWO OF A TRILOGY

Chapter 1

The two mounted policemen rode out of the settlement on an early Spring morning, after a long Winter. Both men were over six feet in height and of a slender build. They were both strong and their faces showed the result of long days in the saddle. The coming Summer would give them both a good tan, wiping the slight pallid effects of Winter. It had been many days since they'd been out riding over the grasslands.

The older of the two men was Ian Percy, who had spent some years in India. His colleague a year or two younger, Bill Todd, had grown up beside the Nepean River, on the eastern side of the Blue mountains. They had teamed up together during the previous Summer finding their combined abilities compatible on the long days on the saddle, also in camp life beside any available waterhole.

Their job was the role of scouting for information on the frontier, under the direction of Sergeant Norm Green. During the late Autumn and Winter they had been required to check all the settlements on the frontier. This enabled them to stay in shelters away from the bad weather. Not all these tents or slab huts were good places to stay, some were little more than bark humpies. Ian was accustomed to washing on a daily basis and found some people had probably not seen a bath for months. Even with his earlier experience of the army in India, he couldn't endure some of the sleeping arrangements.

It was a great relief when Bill received a note from their Sergeant, with instructions to return to the Office at the barracks in the Hill Top settlement. Riding out on a sunny morning, and leaving their most recent settlement, Last Stop, behind, there was a nip of the recent Winter still in the air.

As they rode east from last night's gathering of people, Bill commented, "At least we each received a hot tub last night and we were able to wash our clothes. We're now feeling clean for the first time in weeks."

"I feel almost new again and it's wonderful to be wearing clean clothes."

"I could see you were getting fed up with not being able to wash on a regular basis. I wondered how long you'd be able to stand it before diving into a waterhole." Bill laughed and said.

"I did find living amongst the unwashed and unclean in accommodations difficult. They mightn't have been so bad if they hadn't been so stuffy. I found that part hard to endure."

"At least we got shelter from those bleak winds from the south, Ian."

"Yes we were fortunate to get shelter in mid-Winter. Why are you grinning Bill?" Ian admitted.

"I'm remembering that settlement which we had to visit and you took your swag and slept under a dray. The people thought you were mad and kept away from you."

"We had to leave the next day. The stink in that hut was more than I could endure, I don't know how you stayed in it. Where was the cesspit?" Ian laughed and replied.

"Quite close to the hut, I didn't like the look of it and went bush."

"Do you ever wish you were in a proper house all the time?"

Bill answered after a moment, "I've become accustomed to camping out and seeing new country every day and talking to all kinds of people on the tracks."

"By your words some of my thoughts have entered you."

Bill laughed and replied, "No, you're an extreme case. I'm a mild man and only interested in what's close at hand."

They laughed and a few minutes later Bill mused, "When you die, I think you and your horse will continue to ride over the grasslands, and if anyone sees you, they will wonder why your soul isn't at rest?"

"Do you mean like that legend of the Dutch sea captain?"

"Who?"

"You know the story of the Flying Dutchman who sold his soul in a storm, while sailing around the Cape of Good Hope."

"That's what I meant, it's the same thing riding or sailing."

"Not quite the same Bill."

A silence and then Bill asked, "What was it like when you sailed around the Cape of Good Hope as a sixteen-year-old boy?"

"It's the graveyard of an untold numbers of ships through the centuries. It doesn't surprise me that a sea story arose out of the Cape. The secret is to keep busy doing anything in the ship and never think about the size of the waves."

"You haven't answered my question?"

"No Bill, I was seasick the whole way around the Cape and couldn't have cared less about what was happening to the ship."

"That bad?"

"Yes, on that long trip to India, which was the only time I was really sick."

They rode in silence until Bill spoke quietly, "Odd the thoughts which come into the mind while out here."

Ian smiled and after a little while said "Yes it is. I wonder where the Old Man is?"

"No Ian I don't want to think about him, he sends shivers down my spine. The story of the Dutch Sea Captain, I can think about because he is a legend. The Old Man he is a different 'kettle of fish' altogether."

Ian let the matter drop and asked, "Where did that note say we had to camp on our way to the barracks at Hilltop?"

"You know that valley before the goldfields where we shot those two ducks, and the miner told us we ought to be more considerate."

"I remember and one of our colleagues said he knew a policeman, who would've trampled over his camp for saying those words."

"That camp was close to where we met each other."

"You'd killed a couple of ducks and were cooking them in clay, I saw your campfire and rode down the valley to investigate."

They talked about the beginning of their friendship in the past Summer. In the middle of the afternoon they entered the valley and began to search for the site of their earlier camp.

About midway down the creek, Bill pointed, "There it is, I remember the two old gum trees, because you said there was a beehive up in the branches."

Ian replied, "You said you'd never learnt to climb trees as a boy, when I suggested some honey would go well with the damper!"

They laughed at this memory and chose a site for the camp well away from the swarm of bees high up in the gum tree, at least two hundred yards down the creek.

"I do hope we can get a couple of ducks and a fish because our food supplies are low," Bill said.

While Ian walked quietly down the creek looking for ducks, Bill had taken a line in search of the evening meal. He loved fishing and the silence of watching the play of the water, the ripples at ever widening circles after a bird had swooped down to drink, or a dragonfly that had briefly touched the surface of the water. Catching fish was the secondary activity, he knew it was important to have food, but he did love sitting on the bank of the creek looking at the water, it was so relaxing. Suddenly the quiet was shattered by the sound of a shot and later another one. Ian has found our meat for dinner, Bill thought, smiling.

The friends arrived back in camp with ducks and fish, looking pleased with their hunting abilities. The magpies were taking considerable interest in the camp, as the ducks were guttered followed by the fish. The entrails were discarded several hundred yards away from the campsite. As they had discovered earlier, all kinds of insects, ants and birds had a vested interest in what they had discarded.

Ian found some clay and was happy to take instructions from Bill, until he took over the cooking of the ducks. Ian removed the flat pan from the round leather case hanging beside his saddlebag and prepared the fish. They worked well together, quite accustomed to how each man prepared the camp for the night. Swags out in the open away from overhead branches and a dip under each swag for comfort. The camp's site was all about security, with the swags well away from the fire. Both men were light sleepers out on their patrols and highly observant. Movement of any kind drew their attention, as the sudden flight of birds might mean danger, or if the kangaroos suddenly stood up and were paying attention to something. The bush was always watching, it was alive with constant movement of one kind or another. It was no surprise when Bill looked up at the side of the hill overlooking the valley in the eastly direction, and said slowly, "We've got company."

Ian looked up in the same direction and said with surprise, "What'ya know, I do believe it's our Sergeant Norm Green. What's he doing out here?"

"We're about to find out, Alex is with him and John Hale too."

"I hope they've brought some more rations."

"If they've got more rations, it means we're not going to Hilltop,"

"Who's the horseman behind John?" Ian asked.

"I've never seen him before today."

"Perhaps he's with Alex?"

It was only a short time before the party arrived at the edge of their camp, Sergeant Green surveyed the camp before saying, "You all know Mr. Pitt?"

Bill grinned and said, "I don't think I've ever heard your surname before today Alex."

He also grinned and replied, "Having a short memory Bill, I'm not surprised!"

There was general laughter before the Sergeant interrupted saying, "I don't believe you have met Mr. Baker."

Bill and Ian greeted him and within a few minutes discovered his Chistian name was Steve and he had been brought up in the Rocks area of the city. As with all the men Steve was tall and solidly built and not an ounce of fat on him. There was something about Steve which Bill couldn't place, something different.

The horses were hobbled and John produced more meat, and by the middle of twilight the ducks were cooked, the extra meat was sissling on the fire and there were slices of fish on Ian's flat pan. All this activity was being watched by the six men who knew exactly how they liked their food cooked, with only Bill and Ian liking their meat well done. The other men removed their meat at various times. Neither Alex nor Steve had seen ducks, which were shared, cooked in clay.

Sergeant Green commented, "My late Mother used to cook ducks and fowls in this way and I must say Mr. Todd, you are just as good at it as I remember, you fellows do very well out here."

There were grins all around and Bill replied, "Sergeant we do our best to keep healthy."

With the meal completed there was a general clean up, before several quart-pots were filled with water and put on the fire to make tea. It wasn't long before each man had his mug of the steaming hot brew in hand and only then did the Sergeant speak.

"Mr. Todd, Mr. Percy, no doubt you are wondering what I'm doing out here at this camp?"

Bill answered, "That's a correct assumption Sergeant."

Everyone grinned and the Sergeant actually laughed before saying, "When I think of the problems you two men cause me when you return to Hilltop, it's rather nice to meet you out here, where nothing can go wrong of your making!"

They all knew the stories, except Steve, so a couple were now relayed concerning alcohol and the girls in the lower tent at the settlement, but they were careful to repeat only the versions known to the Sergeant. They were not to know he already knew all the stories! When the humour died down the Sergeant indicated by his hand for Alex to proceed with the briefing.

"As you know, I found Sergeant Rich dead and Bernie and Barry helped me take him to the nearest settlement, which had a cemetery and two graves already in it. We arranged a burial and the visiting Roman Catholic Priest conducted the brief service. We rode at a steady pace, camping one night only, before we located you, Bill and Ian with Fred, at our third stop for the night."

Bill interrupted, "You only found us because Fred's horse tripped and could no longer carry him. Ian's horse had to carry extra weight!"

Alex laughed and said, "I'd be surprised if Ian's horse was even aware of carrying two men."

Sergeant Green commented, "I was thinking you men were old enough to talk about work, without taking a detour into another subject altogether."

"Just clearing up as to why Alex had an easy time finding us," Bill replied, not in the least repentant.

"Have you finished Mr. Todd?"

"Yes Sergeant."

"Good, let us get on with it, Mr. Pitt please."

"At that camp I informed Fred about my suspicions concerning the murder of my Sergeant. Fred told me that you, Sergeant Green, had arranged for him to go to a certain property to learn about being a stockman, and that he would be joined by another policeman, Roy Cook" Alex said.

"Please explain what you did over the late Autumn and Winter months on this matter?" Sergeant Green asked Alex.

"I returned to the city and made a report of what I had seen, keeping my suspicions to myself, until I could be sure it was safe to reveal my thoughts, and Fred's identification of the voice.'

"You were not working on your own were you? I was told you had Mr. Rush assisting you?" the Sergeant asked.

"Mr. Rush?" Bill enquired.

Alex laughed, "Really Bill your memory, it must be because you're getting old!"

Bill gritted his teeth and felt it was a pity that the Sergeant was present.

Ian, looking at Bill in complete understanding, turned to Alex and asked, "Who is Mr. Rush?"

At once he saw grins around the fire and knew it had been a set up.

"Charley!" Alex replied.

The men burst out laughing as Bill expressed his own feelings about the set up in his own language, to their further delight.

"Did you know his surname was Rush?" Bill asked Ian quietly.

"No, nor did I know Alex was Pitt."

"May we proceed gentlemen, if Mr. Todd and Mr. Percy have stopped talking," Sergeant Green asked.

Bill replied, getting his own back, "Yes Sergeant we were just clearing up our memories."

"Good, we are relieved to hear it, please continue and it would be helpful if Mr. Todd refrained from commenting."

Alex grinned at Bill without the Sergeant being aware of it and began to speak.

"When I did make a report about the death and my suspicions, it was dismissed out of hand, I was ordered never to speak of it again."

"Was that the end of it Alex?" Bill asked.

"No. After about ten days I was called to the office of a policeman in another section of the city and was asked to repeat my report in detail, including my suspicions. He was most encouraging and kept me talking. He told me enough about the man, whose name must not be spoken, is a person to be treated with caution."

"What is being done about him?" Ian asked.

"Charley Rush and I moved to this other police district. At the same time some other men moved to this area too, and an operation has begun to investigate the man's activities," Alex said smiling.

"Is he really important in the city?" Bill asked.

"Yes, he's an important merchant and known to be quite ruthless in business. A hard man with criminal connections, not yet proven."

"Do I assume there are now police working on this side of the mountains on this matter?" Ian asked carefully.

"You and Bill have a gift of knowing things unspoken and hidden, and yes there are police operating undercover this side of the mountains," Alex smiled at Ian and added.

Sergeant Green finished drinking his tea and spoke, "I've sent Mr. Hall and Mr. Cook to work on a property in the south. They are being trained as stockmen and learning self-defense tactics." He then added, "I want you Mr. Percy with Mr. Todd to ride down to the property on the western side of the ranges. It is essential for you to be able to recognize Mr. Cook as he may have to contact you some time in the future."

There was silence for a moment or two as Sergeant Green poured himself another mug of tea. Taking a sip and a smiling with satisfaction, he continued, "Your patrol this Summer will include riding north and working near Green Hills, in which the barracks are under the authority of Sergeant Ray Shaw. Mr. Pitt and Mr. Baker will be operating in this area slowly gathering information about the man in question. He is known to be operating a property in that district."

"Are there other police involved in gathering intelligence of which we'll be unaware of their identities?" Ian asked.

"I believe some government agents have an interest in the matter. My only concern is for Mr. Hall and Mr. Cook, who will be under deep cover."

"I'm thinking if Roy comes to us, it will be an emergency and we will act as we see fit at the time," Bill asked in a thoughtful tone of voice.

The Sergeant was quiet for a while before saying, "If this happens, you will act with my authority and I will give a paper to be used whenever something occurs which is unexpected." He added firmly, "Those two men are to have your full protection, you will take them to somewhere safe."

"After meeting up with Fred Hall and Roy Cook, where do we go afterwards?' Ian enquired.

"I expect to see you back at Hill Top to report, and to change your uniforms from Winter to Summer. We will talk later when you return. This meeting is for you to meet Mr. Pitt and Mr. Baker. I'm fully aware you have both had working experience with Mr. Pitt. It is important for you to know Mr. Baker, so if you meet again no explanations will be required."

"Where are you going in the morning, Sergeant?" Ian asked.

"Mr. Hale and I will be returning to Hill Top, Mr. Pitt and Mr. Baker will proceed north to work under the authority of Sergeant Shaw. For these two policemen, this is a special assignment, and never to be spoken about in any context. Is that understood gentlemen?"

A chorus of voices, "Yes Sergeant."

They all went to their swags after Bill put out the fire with a quart-pot of water. With so many police in the camp, Bill and Ian had put their swags close together so they could talk as usual. It had been an interesting evening. Neither Bill nor Ian had noticed that John had put his swag within talking distance of Steve's swag.

Steve had seen Bill and Ian's swags and asked John, "Why so close John?"

"They talk quietly into the night, concerning whatever is on their minds at the end of the day."

"They act like brothers."

John laughed and said, "Just about could be Steve!"

"Trustworthy?"

"Yes and won't hesitate if you're in trouble."

"Good to know.'

John asked carefully "What did you do before joining the police?"

"Roy and I were prize fighters and attached to a group of men who roamed the streets in our part of the city. We know how to look after ourselves in tight places. We both hate evil men who prey on the weak and powerless."

John and Steve talked quietly, while at the other side of the camp Bill and Ian were talking about the recent meeting.

"I have the feeling there is a lot more to these plans which our Sergeant is keeping to himself," Ian suggested

"I thought the same as if he was deciding how much to tell us?"

"So we both think alike."

"You know we do! How did Steve strike you?"

"By the look of his shoulders and arm muscles and the size of his hands, I'd say he would be quite able to take care of himself in a fight, I'd want him on my side!"

"Good to know, what did Alex tell you about him?"

"He grew up in the Rocks part of the city and can recognize criminal activities almost before they happen!"

Ian laughed and said, "In other words just like us. I liked him and his straight way of talking."

They talked for a while and other voices faded into silence. When Ian turned to face the creek, the only sounds were coming from the treetops. Curious animals moved away from the silent sleeping forms near the trees. The only other sound was the movement of the horses and the tinkling of their hobbles. Ian loved to hear this chorus of the night life and stayed awake just to listen to it. Until at last his eyes closed and the night faded…

Chapter 2

Before sunrise the camp was stirring with Ian making his way down to the creek to wash on a chilly crisp morning. He was watched by Steve, before following Ian. No words were spoken as each man wiped away sleep in cold water.

"Do you always wash?" Steve asked quietly.

"Yes, because I like to feel clean and in the hot months it's full immersion."

No other words were spoken for several minutes before Ian spoke, "Have you done any prize fighting?"

"Is it that obvious?"

"Yes, you have the figure of a man who knows how to look after himself and the scars to prove it."

"John Hale told me you and Bill were highly observant."

"Have you known John for long?"

"Yes for most of the Winter. I've had to learn to ride a horse."

"How's it going? Have you been bucked off a few times?" Ian smiled at him.

"Slowly, yes I've come off a few times. I'm accustomed to street fighting and being on a horse all day is hard going most days. John is a good teacher and has never given up at my slow learning ability," Steve replied.

"John would look after you regardless of how badly you rode your horse, I suspect you would never give in either."

"You're correct. Roy and I never give in to our weaknesses. John is a nice man, except he will talk at breakfast."

"That is of course, his downfall. One look at Bill today and he'll be silent, you watch," Ian laughed.

They walked back to the camp in silence to see John making the fire in silence after a glance from Bill. Steve smiled to himself. The meal was eaten in silence until John said in surprise, "We have visitors."

Bill looked up at the opposite hill and exclaimed, "It's not appreciated at this time of the morning."

"Bill you can't always have your own way," John laughed as Bill voiced his opinion.

"Can't I?"

"No. I've never known such a gloomy lot of men as you, Ian and Steve on an early sunny morning when all of nature is waking up. Listen to the birds singing, they are happy."

Alex saw an expression on the Sergeant's face, which put him in the same mind as Ian and company.

When Alex laughed Ian asked, "What's funny Alex?"

"All of us love silence at breakfast except John who is a morning person. It requires a great deal of understanding on John's part to remain silent in the mornings, but we make no effort to remain silent late at night."

"Majority rules and we do make allowances for John at night. Sometimes," Ian said quietly.

While he was speaking they were all watching the approach of the two mounted policemen, now riding across the floor of the valley.

"James Wade and George Nash, I wonder what they are doing here?" John said identifying them.

The Sergeant stood up and walked to meet the men who both men alighted from their horses. George walked forward and handed a paper to his Sergeant.

"This arrived for you about two hours after you had left Hill Top. I was told that it was vital that you received it as soon as possible, so we followed you," he said.

"Have you eaten today?" John asked.

"No. We camped last night after dark and left again before dawn, to reach you before you left here," James said.

John set about preparing more food. George walked to the fire and warmed his hands while talking to Ian about the recent ride.

The Sergeant read the paper then said, "A change in our plans. This note says in part that information has been received that the man in question has an exceptional memory, which means Mr. Hall, cannot be involved as we had planned. Mr. Baker you will have to join Mr. Cook. The note informs me that you know what the man looks like and can identify him?"

"Yes Sergeant, both Roy and I can identify him. We've seen him up close."

As Steve was speaking his voice changed from his normal friendly one to a cold hard one.

"Mr. Baker are you happy to join Roy Cook in this training program?" the Sergeant asked.

"Yes Sergeant. Roy is like a brother to me, we have looked out for one another since we were children. We've been in some tight places over the years and have always managed to escape danger."

"Thank you. From what I've seen and heard of you I'm happy to let you take up this appointment. Mr. Percy and Mr. Todd will escort you down to the property. Do you need anything?"

"No Sergeant, except where do I change into my Summer uniform?"

"You won't need it because you're going undercover. I understand you have with you some old clothes to wear when required?"

"Yes Sergeant."

"I suggest you change here and I'll take your Winter uniform back to my barracks. When the time is right, I will see you get your Summer one."

Ian who was listening suggested, "Sergeant, the weather is still cold in the early mornings and Steve will be riding his police marked horse. Why not let him continue in his winter uniform to the property. We'll bring his horse back to Hilltop, and use it as a packhorse with his gear attached to it?"

Sergeant Green smiled and replied, "I had forgotten about his police horse. That's a capital idea Mr. Percy, also the saddle, is it police issue too?"

"Yes Sergeant all the equipment is police owned," Steve replied.

"Good. It all must come back to the barracks. Mr. Baker you must check that nothing in any way connects you to the police. Regardless send it back to me. Are you happy with this arrangement?"

"Yes Sergeant, I do feel the cold up in these hills. It's warmer on the coast and I'd like to keep my winter uniform for a bit longer if possible?"

"Right you can keep it to ride to the property,"

"Thank you Sergeant. How long will I be at there?"

"This is a decision which will be made on the site, you'll be trained to be stockman."

"It may be weeks, because this experience of riding and stockwork is new to me."

"None of your colleagues present except for James, has ever done stockwork, but we have spent days in the saddle, after Mr. Hale learnt to stay on his horse!"

There was laughter which put Steve at ease.

Later he asked John, "Did it really take you a long time to learn to ride a horse?"

"Yes it did and I had to put up with all their humour at my expense. This made me more determined to succeed in riding my horse."

There seemed to be no hurry to break camp, while George and James ate a well-prepared meal. They had pushed their horses to reach this site and now were quite happy to sit by a fire and talk to friends. First it was George who stopped speaking, walked over to an open space, lay down and went to sleep. James did the same on another patch of bare grass. Their friends didn't intrude anywhere near them, walking away up the creek they found some logs on the bank and sat down to talk.

"Who is to accompany me going northwards Sergeant?" Alex asked.

"Mr. Hale will go with you and remain with you until this matter is resolved one way or another."

"Sergeant do you have any definite instructions?" John enquired

"Yes Mr. Hale, even though Mr. Pitt has had country experiences, he is a city policeman. You and Mr. Pitt will work together and Sergeant Shaw is aware of my request on this matter."

Alex grinned at John and drawled, "It appears we'll be doing other work and at the same time gathering intelligence,"

"I suppose so, we'll be learning from each other about different styles of police work. Do you talk at breakfast?" John replied in the same tone of voice.

"If I must!"

Laughter and Bill declared, "You've lost that one John!"

"If Alex is a night owl he'll be on his own."

"We'll find a compromise because we're friends," Alex suggested.

The Sergeant spoke firmly as only a man of his rank was accustomed to do so at any time, which caused instant obedience.

"I'll give Mr. Nash and Mr. Wade another hours sleep. They can accompany me back to my barracks today."

Bill made a comment about their food saying, "We need meat and will try and find a young kangaroo. The weather is cool enough to carry meat for a couple of days. I noticed watercress growing in the creek, it will give us a balanced diet for today."

Steve asked carefully, "What is watercress?"

Ian replied grinning, "Probably akin to seaweed!"

The men laughed seeing Steve's expression.

"Steve it's like a water vegetable and isn't too bad to eat." Alex explained, taking mercy on him.

After the general humour died down, the men stood up and walked back to the camp.

Bill handed over a quantity of food to Alex saying, "We'll replenish our supplies before we ride south, you take this meat."

"Are you sure Bill?"

"Yes Alex and look after yourselves."

"We will."

John and Alex left the camp and rode up the valley and in a short period of time were out of sight over the crest of the hill. The Sergeant had been standing out on the grass away from the creek to watch the men depart.

"It's better being in my Office, I'm sending those two men into trouble and I can do nothing for them. It's hard being the Sergeant," he said to Bill.

"Those two men are our friends and I wouldn't want either of them searching for me. They are both cunning and can make instant decisions."

"Are you sure?"

"Yes Sergeant, John always scrapes through any job he does out on the frontier He might get a scratch or two but he never lets go once he's on the scent of his quarry. Alex is also a tough man."

"In this case I do hope he knows when to retreat and when to catch a crook?"

"As I've said, Alex Pitt is a steady hand and will stand by him. They'll be okay Sergeant."

"One day Mr. Todd, you will be a sergeant and you'll know what it's like sending men out on jobs, knowing some may not return home, and a letter will have to be written."

"We understand the risks Sergeant, it goes with being a policeman. The frontier needs men who are prepared to give encouragement to those seeking a better life."

They talked as the Sergeant turned around and walked back into the camp to see if James Wade was awake and watched him walk across and nudge his colleague with his boot. Now refreshed, their horses saddled again, they mounted and rode out of the valley behind their Sergeant.

Chapter 3

Steve watched the Sergeant and the two policemen leave, and standing beside Ian asked, "What do we do now?"

"You and I are going hunting for meat and Bill's going to try and catch a fish for the evening meal."

"What sort of meat?"

"A young kangaroo is good eating."

"If you say so?" Steve replied uncertainly.

"Steve, there aren't too many choices out on the frontier when our rations are low. We eat a lot of fish and damper and sometimes we get wild honey. Our diet needs meat too," Ian laughed and replied.

"What about vegetables?" Steve asked.

"Bill mentioned watercress, an acquired taste and better than nothing. We buy from the settlers and eat vegetables at every opportunity."

They walked in silence for about two hundred yards, before Ian spoke quietly, "Steve you'll become accustomed to rough living as a stockman, kangaroo meat will be your main diet. Sheep and cattle are too valuable to kill. The only time you will get it is if the animal breaks a leg or has some accident, even then you might not get it if it can be sold?"

Steve listened carefully before saying, "Both Roy and I grew up in hard conditions where food was never wasted and we frequently went to bed hungry. Roy lived next door to me until we were turned out into the street. There was no one to care for us, until a woman of the streets gave us a bed. We had to get out when she had a client, but she sent us to school and paid the few shillings for our education."

"I've heard you talk about the Rocks district, what does it mean?"

"One of the poor parts of the city, probably one of the major crime areas. Roy and I have seen all kinds of crime, we were little more than street urchins when she was working, we grew up with an abiding hatred of those who prey on the weak and defenseless, particularly the man who we are seeking."

Ian suddenly stopped walking and grasped Steve's arm, pulling him down amongst the tall grass.

"Look up ahead?" he said quietly.

A number of kangaroos were feeding, with an older one standing high keeping an eye out for danger. The men had been seen approaching and the kangaroo was now standing up assessing the situation.

"Never get too close to these animals, they're quite capable of splitting you open with their claws," Ian cautioned.

"They're lovely to look at."

"I love to see them too, but now we need meat."

Ian raised his rifle and fired at a medium sized animal and killed it instantly while all the others hopped away. Spears they knew but not bullets…..Men were a danger and their curiosity wasn't helpful to their survival when food was required. Ian and Steve walked forward to retrieve the catch.

"Steve always kill in a way that the animal doesn't suffer too much pain. I kill for food and never for my pleasure," Ian advised.

"I think the hunters would disagree with you."

"We who ride the grasslands love the wildlife and it'll be a grim life if they all disappear."

As they were talking Ian skinned it and removed those parts that were not required. Steve began to notice the number of birds gathering on the branches above his head and taking an interest in what Ian was doing.

"What kind of bird is it?" he asked.

"I thought you would know Steve."

"No. I've seen them since coming here and haven't paid much attention until now."

"Magpies. They sing in the mornings, you must have heard their voices?"

"I'll listen when I wake up tomorrow."

Ian gathered up the required meat into a bag and began to walk back to the camp. Behind them there was a flutter of wings as the birds of prey descended upon the discarded food, Steve turned and watched for a moment or two, then turned and walked beside Ian.

"There was a time Ian, when Roy and I would've done what the birds are doing now," he mused quietly.

Ian wasn't shocked, surprised perhaps, he'd seen enough of the world to understand what being poor was all about, eating what others discarded to survive, just like the birds of prey.

"Do you and Roy still see the woman who looked after you when you were young?" Ian asked.

Steve smiled and replied. "Yes we do, we made money prize fighting and moved her out of the street where she rented a large room. We made enough money to rent a small shop for her to run a tearoom. We have become her family. We don't ask questions about her life, we just accept her as we have always done."

"So she could be still in the game?"

"Yes and Roy thinks a better type of men, after all this is the life she knows well."

"You really don't mind do you?"

"No Ian, without her we wouldn't be police today, nor would we have had a reasonable education. We do keep an eye on her and would go to her aid in a flash, if she needed us. You don't approve Ian?"

"It isn't that Steve, it's because of possible danger, we both know there are some men who like to hurt women?"

"We're aware of that possibility and have arranged for a man to keep an eye on her."

"Do you plan to move her if you and Roy stay on this side of the mountains?"

"Yes we do and we've talked about it with her and she'll come to live with one of us.'

They talked about this matter on the way back to the camp, where Ian began to cook the meat.

"We cook the meat rare to carry for the next couple of days, we then cook it properly. Both Bill and I like well cooked meat and this way it lasts longer than any other way of preparing it," Ian explained.

"I like my meat well-cooked too," Steve said.

As they talked Steve enquired, "What did Bill do before joining the police?"

"He worked on the site of a brick-kiln and later in a shop. Were you and Roy always in the fighting game?'

"No, before joining we did some months on a construction site, we thought this occupation might look better on paper!"

"I believe you were correct in your assessment of what looked better on paper! Your knowledge of fighting is also a requirement in our job," Ian replied.

The meat was well on the way to being cooked by the time Bill returned with a large fish.

"I could smell the meat cooking a fair distance up the creek, if there's anyone near us we'll very likely have a visitor wanting food," he said.

"Is that a normal reaction to the smell of cooking meat?" Steve asked.

"Food isn't plentiful on the frontier, unless a man has money or gold," Bill replied.

No one disturbed them that night and early next morning before sunrise, they rode out of the valley. At the top of the hill, the first rays of the sun touched the highest branches of the trees. In this light the birds began to chatter, creating the songs of the morning. It was a beautiful day with a light dew on the grass and massive areas of wildflowers growing everywhere around them, like a great big garden for miles in every direction. Ian looked down at the horses hooves as they walked through this garden. He gave up asking Bill about the names of the wildflowers, after a few 'I don't know Ian' and

'Don't ask.'

Steve rode in silence and seemed to be amused as his two colleagues carried on a conversation. There was a wide-open space with nothing in sight when

Bill's horse suddenly stopped. Ian and Steve's horses followed suit and began to walk backwards, their heads up and ears straight as if listening to some sound which was beyond the range of their riders.

"Right, we'll back away from whatever is here. The horses will guide us around the problem," Ian suggested

As with all the other times, the horses did a wide turn and walked in another direction away from that area of ground. Steve followed the two men or at least his horse did.

After a little while he enquired, "What was wrong with the horses?"

"You tell him," Bill said to Ian.

"Alright, but you could tell Steve."

"No, you tell him!"

Steve laughed and asked, "So who is going to tell me?"

Ian turned on his saddle towards Steve and began to speak.

"Steve this land looks empty, but it isn't quite what it seems. The earlier people who roamed these grasslands now seem like black shadows of the past and move quietly away from us to avoid problems."

"I know about them, so why did the horse shy?"

"There are lots of sites where animals refuse to go, we have no knowledge of the ancient stories of what had taken place on these sites. We show respect by not forcing our horses to ride on them,"

"But what do you think is there?"

"We have an ancient friend whom we call the Old Man, who is of this race of people, he would say for us to keep away from these places," Ian explained

"There could have been a fight ending in death and their spirit is still here," Bill added.

"This isn't an entirely new experience for me. Roy and I had a friend and he told us some strange stories too," Steve said quietly.

"These people owned this land, their stories cover it and one day perhaps we may earn some of their history too," Ian mused.

Steve remained silent as they rode south up out of the valley.

"Are you okay Steve?" Bill finally asked him.

"I don't cope well with things I can't see, but I know there are aspects of this land which will always be unknown. It's a new experience with the horses and I find this disturbing."

"Steve we would never camp near one of those places. We treat them with respect," Ian added.

"So you are saying these places are real?"

"Yes, I believe the shadow people observe us and continue to honour their ancient beliefs and it will always be secret from us."

"But why Ian?"

"We destroy what we don't understand."

"What you're saying is that we are under observation and you don't mind?" Steve said.

"We're frequently under observation as we ride between the settlements, goldfields and squatters. We're rarely alone, regardless of who is seeing us, ancient people or the new people," Ian smiled and replied.

Bill picked up from Ian's words and continued, "We're observed by lots of people, but very few will come to our aid in times of trouble, in this sense we are really on our own out here."

They talked about being alone and Steve explained about an aspect of his past, saying, "We found, as children, that being alone together we were safe. Being with police colleagues out here is also safe, I wouldn't like to be on my own."

Ian lent over and prodded Steve on the shoulder.

"Steve you could give a good account of yourself in any confrontation by yourself or in company," Ian commented. "I'm sorry Steve, we're talking about being alone, when you and Roy will soon be going undercover, and you will be on your own. Always treat the shadow people with respect and never hinder them in your work."

"That's alright Ian, this a learning period for me."

They were riding three abreast where possible and Steve tried to stop daydreaming about what Roy might be doing, or what they would be facing undercover.

Bill and Ian were teaching him, all the time riding south. They also avoided doing any police work on the ride to keep Steve safe, the fewer people who saw him the better for his survival.

The property they were seeking was on the edge of the south-east ranges. These were the same ranges which they had ridden through last Summer. Ian was interested in the directions which indicated a ride down the western side of the range. He expected to see the beginning of the ranges, perhaps late on the afternoon of the next day. They camped beside a creek with a fast-flowing stream. There must have been a storm in the catchment area to create this minor flood.

"Can you swim?" Ian asked Steve looking at the fast-flowing stream.

"Yes, Roy and I learnt to swim when we were quite young, we were close to the sea as you know. Bad men, when they were drunk, tossed little kids into the water to see if they could swim. Some didn't get out alive."

Bill, who was gathering wood, stopped and asked, "Did anyone ever stop them?"

"Only if they were bigger and stronger."

Ian remembered an earlier comment made by Steve about the man they would be investigating.

"What do you know about the man from the city whom you and Roy will be investigating undercover?" he asked.

Steve actually paled and seemed to gather himself together before saying, "Roy and I witnessed a shocking scene when we were called by his men to attend a demonstration of obedience to that man. Not just us but all our mates from the streets. We were close to the edge of the water and could clearly see what he did."

"Steve, if you don't want to talk about it, you don't have to speak about a bad memory," Bill interrupted.

"I know Bill, but I'd like you and Ian to know where I'm coming from to do this job."

"As long as you are happy to go ahead Steve," Ian commented.

"As I said, we were close enough to see he was feeding two sharks and we wondered why we'd been called to watch him. Suddenly a man was thrust forward to the edge of the water. He was a friend to all the children and had refused to cooperate with the man. We'd always known him, he'd sold sweets to us kids and when we didn't have any money, he'd give us the sweets, he was a kind man. I think we knew what was about to happen. Words were spoken and he was pushed into the sea. We heard his cries of agony, before he was pulled under the water. The man made it plain this was the result of not cooperating with him."

Bill and Ian were not entirely shocked, as this form of punishment was used by criminals living in various areas close to the sea. It was a case of understanding why Steve and Roy wanted to catch this evil man and take him out of circulation. They both felt compassion for Steve's unpleasant memory. Bill left Ian to make the fire and walked up beside Steve. They walked down the creek and Bill told him he wasn't alone in his grief.

He explained that people did evil deeds and their work as police was to try to protect the people who wanted to live in peace.

"I left the work at the brick-kiln after a horrid event, one of my work mates had won a sum of money from the foreman. This man didn't like being beaten and accused my mate of cheating. The foreman wanted his money back, my mate refused, he'd won it fair and square. The foreman organized a couple of his friends to tie him up and gag him, they put him in the kiln and bricked up the entrance. Two days later they let him out," Bill said.

"What happened to him?" Steve asked quietly.

"No one knows, he walked out of the yard on that day. We heard he gathered his family and left the city. On that same day, I picked up what was owing to me and left that job."

"Is that when you got a job in a shop?"

"Yes and from there to the police."

Back at the fire Bill recounted this story to Ian who commented, "That man will suffer nightmares all his life about being bricked-up in the kiln, at any moment a fire could have been started, it was a cruel act."

They talked about it until Ian said, "I think we ought to fill our minds with happy thoughts until the fire dies down, or we'll all have nightmares!"

Steve heartily approved and Bill recounted some police stories, which caused fits of laughter then each of them retired feeling it had been a good day.

*

Steve woke up in the morning after a long sleep and was surprised to discovered he was the last one up, then walked down to the creek to wash. Ian was already in the creek washing himself and was naked from the waist up. Steve was surprised to note Ian wasn't a white man, he'd assumed that his face was tanned from long days in the saddle. He thought Ian was very like himself with powerful shoulders and arms. Bill had washed earlier and was now cooking breakfast when Steve walked back to the camp, leaving Ian in the creek.

"What's Ian's background, I've seen him in the creek?" Steve asked quietly.

Bill looked up from the fire where he had been arranging the quart-pots.

"Ian has inherited the colour of his great grandmother who was a Spanish Lady. He is fortunate that he doesn't get sunburnt and will develop a dark tan in Summer," he replied.

Steve began to feel uncomfortable and Bill noted his unease.

"Ian was a shock to me when I first saw him fully naked swimming in the creek. Since then, I've come to think of him like a brother. To me that's all that matters," he said quietly.

Steve smiled and spoke, "Those words are more valuable than any money. What Ian is to you, Roy is to me."

Ian returned from a most satisfying wash in the creek and enquired, "What are you talking about looking so earnestly into the fire?"

Bil looked up, smiled and replied, "Friendship."

Ian looked at Steve and asked, "Roy?"

Rather surprised Steve asked, "How did you know?"

"The story you told last night. When you spoke of Roy you talked about him like a brother." There was silence before Ian added, "Steve no one can exist on their own."

Before Ian could continue his story, Bill chipped in saying with a grin, "That's when I found Ian wandering around on his own!"

For once they had a breakfast with humour, instead of the usual grim silence. They realized Steve was going through a major change in becoming an undercover policeman. It was a mindset and would gradually come to take over his life. After the meal and all packed, they followed the creek until the sun was overhead.

"We need to ride to the top of the nearest high hill to get our bearings again," Bill suggested.

"What about that one up ahead of us?" Ian said pointing with his hand.

"I think the hill a little to the east of us is higher than your one Ian?" Steve suggested thoughtfully.

His two colleagues smiled, they were riding out in front of Steve and he was unaware of their humour.

"I think Steve is correct, it does look higher. We'll go there and see where we are situated?" Bill replied.

Ian led the way and within a short period of time they were climbing the hill. Walking one way, turning and walking up another way, steadily going up through the trees and crossing gullies. Ian looked out across the valleys, now high above them, the views across the landscape were magnificent in all directions. He turned his horse this way and that so as not to miss seeing any part of it.

"Ian can gaze at these views forever, he loves the grandeur of the landscape on the frontier," Bill spoke quietly to Steve.

Ian turned in his saddle and expressed, "This is a new land to me Steve, and I do love all aspects of it, from the ancient ones to the wide-open spaces, it's full of story, if only we have the time to listen to the wind in the trees. Bill takes it for granted, or at least he did, until he met me."

"Steve I had no option in the matter!" Bill laughed and added.

Ian addressed Steve, "When you think of your cramped city streets and buildings so close together, now you are out in an isolated world, gazing at the wonders of nature. Wild animals, brightly coloured birds, isn't good to be here?"

Steve looked at Ian's face, alight with the joy of being alive, and with Ian's words singing in his head, he wished his friend Roy was here too.

"Ian, as you say this is a new land for you and you see it with new eyes. I'd say you were country bred, you'd have to be to love this land. My youth was spent on narrow streets and the cobblestones speak to my feet. The sharp corners, narrow lanes where we once played or ran for our lives, the smell of woodfires and coal dust are all home to me."

Ian rode for a while in silence along the top of the hill, before saying, "To each his own Steve. If the city streets call you back at the end of this assignment, so be it and once again you will be enfolded in your world,"

Steve rode in silence as he digested Ian's words, there were great possibilities here, he felt there were so many ideas to pass on to Roy. They'd talk about them one day. He sat slightly forward on his saddle as he plodded along behind Bill and Ian, daydreaming about all these new ideas and how Roy might respond to them. The silence continued as they crossed the valley towards a bank of tall gum trees, which indicated a creek. Bill was the first one to see what was in front of them.

"We have a problem," he said.

"What is it?" Steve asked.

"You can hear it, the creek is in flood and we have to cross it," Bill replied.

"This isn't the weather to get wringing wet," Ian groaned expressing his thoughts.

"It's a clear sky, isn't it Ian?" Steve stated, not yet understanding what Ian was saying.

"He's right, it is a clear sky," Bill cheerfully acknowledged

"And very wet low down, Bill."

They rode carefully to the edge of the water, it was fast flowing and the banks on the other side of the creek were high.

"What do you think Bill?" Ian asked.

"We can't cross here, there are no visible tracks made by animals to show they've crossed anywhere near here."

"So we ride which way?" Ian queried.

"I'd ride towards the ranges."

They were constantly seeking animal tracks as they rode along in sight of the water. In some low-lying places the water had spread out into the valley, indicating a heavy storm had fallen somewhere in the east. The horses were also keeping a watch out for snakes, which were dislodged by the flood, from their hibernation. Flood waters had a habit of bringing all kinds of things to the surface, in many instances live creatures, willing to grasp anything above the water. Some bite when they are dislodged, as the men had discovered in earlier crossings.

At last they found a solid path made by animals and it led to a flat area beside the creek, where the banks were low enough for the horses to climb out of the water.

"If we enter the water here, the current of the flood water will take us down the creek for a little way and we ought to be able to get out of the water where the banks are low," Bill explained to Steve, pointing with his hand at the low part.

"You need to talk to Steve about the horses, we don't know about his horse," Ian suggested to Bill.

"No, we don't know."

"I don't understand, why would my horse be any different from your horses?" Steve asked, feeling uneasy.

"Steve, the horses don't like the flooded creeks any more than we do. They're strong swimmers and the current pushes them downstream, this is why we choose low banks to get out of the water. Not only is the horse swimming, but we are on their backs too, so whatever you do don't let go of the reins. Sometimes a horse will slip and roll, you stay on, because the horse will come up again as quickly as possible," Bill began to explain carefully.

Ian took up the lesson, "We know our horses are strong swimmers, but your horse is unknown. Some horses can't swim, they walk along the bottom of the creek and drown, not often but sometimes."

"This is why we'll be riding close to you when we enter the water. Once your horse starts to swim we'll be contented to let you go on your own beside us. Don't be concerned if the current pulls you away from us, just aim for the low bank," Bill continued.

"So I give my horse his head to make his own decision?" Steve asked.

"Correct," Bill smiled an answered.

"You told us you could swim?" Ian asked, just to make sure.

"Yes, I can keep my head above water."

"Even dressed and with your boots on?" Ian grinned.

"No problem, slower perhaps," Steve replied.

In the silence after giving his answer Steve suddenly asked, "Can we go and get it over and done with? I'll be okay."

Both men laughed and Ian said, "Bill you lead the way."

They rode to the place on the bank which Bill had suggested as the best track to enter the flooded creek. The horses didn't balk at entering the flood water. As Bill had indicated their horses were strong swimmers and it was a relief when Steve's horse showed no discomfort in the water. The current was strong and it did carry the horses down the stream to the lower banks about a hundred yards from where they'd entered the water. Climbing up the bank and on to dry land with water dripping from their saddles and clothes, the men were aware their boots were full of water. Their swags were also drenched. On a bare and dry patch of ground the men alighted from their horses, removed their boots and poured out the water. None of them spoke a word about their condition. Bill and Ian put their boots on again and mounted and continued to ride in an eastly direction.

"We need to find a suitable place to camp, well protected from a cold breeze," Bill finally said.

"We'll need the sunlight as well as a couple of fires to dry out our clothes. We're in for a couple of uncomfortable hours," Ian stated.

Steve questioned Ian who explained, "Steve, we can't afford to wear wet clothes at all, this isn't a place to get sick. Regardless of the climate we strip off our heavy clothing and sit in front of the best fire we make to keep us warm."

"Oh! Is that what now happens?"

"Yes Steve, we don't have any other option."

"Will this happen in a stock camp?" he asked.

Bill saw that Steve was a bit disturbed about stripping off his clothes to get dry.

"It will depend upon how relaxed you are with those men in your camp, with some men not at all, and others will be okay. It's about keeping good health," he answered carefully.

They continued to ride beside the creek, before crossing the hill, which showed they were quite close to the ranges. In this part of the ride they had left the flooded creek and entered another valley, which they'd seen from the top of the hill. Bill decided to find a place to camp. There was a small creek with flowing fresh water, which was entirely suitable for their need of drinking water.

Bill pointed at the curve in the creek and suggested, "I can see some big logs out on the bank of the creek, what do you think?"

Ian rode forward to look at the large old logs, which were wide enough for the men to build several fires in between them

"We can make three fires in a line, and hammer sticks into the ground to spread our clothes to get the best of the sunlight and the heat of the fire," Bill suggested.

"I like dry clothes and anything which produces that happy condition is okay by me," Ian replied.

It didn't take long to strip their horses of the saddles and cloths. The best positions for the saddle cloths were given to them to dry, as care of the horses always took priority over other considerations, like drying their own clothes.

"This is hardly the weather to strip and sit in front of a fire, but my desire for dry clothes wins the day," Ian commented.

Around the fire the men watched the steam rise from their wet clothes, the horse saddle cloths and their swags.

"We're in for an uncomfortable night, there is no other way to describe it in our experience after crossing a flooded river or creek. Our clothes will be damp, the light garments might be bone dry, depending upon when we start the fire. Rations and most things in our saddle bags are all wet. We save what we can use until we get fresh supplies." Bill said, glancing at Steve.

"Do you mean to say that not only do we have to endure a cold afternoon sitting in our underwear beside a creek, but when we get dressed again it will be in damp clothes," Steve asked.

"That's the way of dealing with the problems we endure out on patrol," Bill was amused and replied.

"But you make every effort to dry the saddle cloths over our wellbeing," Steve said.

"The welfare of our horses are vital to us," Bill said, before adding cheerfully, "Ride in comfort or walk in discomfort."

"I do see the need to look after the horses," Steve reluctantly agreed.

Ian who had listened to the conversation explained, "I learnt that lesson the hard way a long time ago. I thought I was more important than my horse. The walk home took all day at a fast pace. Now my horse is my most precious possession."

"Is that why you hobble them at night?"

"We hobble them at night, so Ian won't have to run for miles to find his horse in the morning!" Bill replied.

"It's the other way round Steve, Bill likes to find his horse close at hand!" Ian laughed and said.

"Is that the only reason?"

"If there was a stallion near we'd lose our horses or an emergency, we can always ride if the horses have been hobbled for the night," Ian answered. He smiled and asked, "Steve if a pretty girl suddenly put in an appearance, would you stay with us or go and investigate?'

"In an instant, before you'd seen her," he laughed and answered.

"What makes you think mares are any different?"

"We need to put more wood on the fires and turn the clothes over, Ian you do the saddle cloths," Bill interrupted.

They set about making the changes and ensuring the fires burned well and soon forgot their own discomfort. Their underclothes were soon dry and as the hours progressed into the night, they were able to slowly dress, except their boots which were still damp in the morning. It had not mattered that the meat was wet and Ian had cooked it both at night and in the morning. Eating the hot food made all the difference to how they felt in this uncomfortable camp.

There was silence as the sun rose in the eastern sky and it would be a few hours before it penetrated the camp site, by that time they would have left. The men enjoyed mugs of hot tea, a little worse for wear after being soaked in the flood water. No man even spoke of the different taste, it was hot that was all that mattered. In the continued silence the men mounted their horses and rode east. Slowly the distant ranges grew in size and by mid-afternoon they reached the high hills. They continued down the western side on the lookout for a squatter's hut, to ask about the whereabouts of Red Bryant's land. Just inside the curve of a heavily wooded hill Bill spied a hut, almost hidden in the undergrowth.

They rode forward a little way and stopped as Ian suggested, "If we all go it might make whoever is there afraid. You go Bill and ask our question."

As Bill rode forward towards the small slab hut, Steve said, "Red is a funny Christian name."

"I don't know his Christian name, he's called Red because he has a red hair and a beard," Ian replied

Meanwhile as Bill rode close to the hut a dog barked and a young man came out from behind the hut, carrying a rifle. Bill remained on his horse and asked the question.

The young man said, "You can't be up to no good if you are going to Red's place?'

"You're right, we're police"

"Not the usually clean looking police?"

"No, we've been in a flooded creek."

"You look it!"

"Where is Red's place?"

"Is he in trouble with the law?"

"No, we're making a delivery."

"I hope you're being truthful, he's a good neighbour. It's the next open valley down a couple of miles away. You'll see some yards and several slab huts and one bigger than the other ones. That's Red Bryant's place."

After thanking him, Bill turned and rode back to where Ian and Steve were waiting with their horses chewing on the grass. Bill passed on the details of Red's place. It was a comfortable ride down beside the great hills rising up east of them. In the west it was mostly flat grasslands, stretching for miles out to the horizon.

Chapter 4

There was no doubt they'd arrived at the correct destination, when a tall well-built man with bright red hair and a long red beard walked forward from near one of the huts and greeted them with a big smile on his face.

"So you're here at last. I was expecting you last week."

"We're here now," Ian introduced Steve and Bill.

"I'm Red, to everyone. By the look of you I'd say you've been across a flooded creek?" Red Bryant said cheerfully.

"Yes yesterday, water over our saddles," Ian replied.

"You can use this one while you're staying here. I'd suggest you put your saddles and cloths along the top of this wooden fence to help them dry properly," Red said, leading the way to one of the slab huts. When you've done your normal jobs, come across to my hut and we can have a talk."

"Are Roy or Fred here?" Steve asked.

Red looked hard at Steve and replied, "They'll be back here before nightfall. Roy has talked about you and has told me what you'd witnessed as young kids. You'll get all the help from me that I can give you. I can help you because I did undercover work when I was in the police."

"Sergeant Green didn't tell us that small detail Red," Ian smiled and spoke quietly.

"Did he tell you that we trained together?"

"No not a word. You were a policeman?"

"Yes a long time ago, now I'm a squatter and it's a good life."

With this new knowledge, they unsaddled their horses and put the damp equipment along the top of the wooden fence as Red had suggested, this included their swags rolled out in the sun. The interior of the slab hut was basic, as expected, places for the swags of three men, a log table sawn flat along the top and several stumps around it for seats. A place for a fire outside the hut, away from the wooden walls. Down the hill was a creek for washing. The track was well worn, which indicated that buckets of water were carried up to the main cooking area every day. At last they completed brushing down their horses, let them out into the paddock with the other horses and secured the gate. It was time to walk across to Red's hut, which was a large hut with additions, set back amongst the trees with a yard behind it and another slab hut. Red came out to greet them and pointed at this other hut to Steve.

"That's where your friends Roy and Fred are camped," he said.

Ian had noticed the whole set up of this property was well organised, neat and tidy. The yards were also of a well-planned design, all round quite impressive.

"I wonder why he left the police?" Bill asked.

"I don't think we can ask that question," Ian mused.

"No perhaps not, though I'm curious about his undercover work."

"Perhaps that's why he'll be training Roy and myself because he's been in our position and will know the pit falls of this work," Steve said.

In an instant Bill and Ian stopped walking and turned to face Steve.

"Now this appointment is beginning to make sense, what do you think Ian?" Bill speculated.

"Steve, feel free to ask Red anything you feel like knowing about this undercover work. We don't have the freedom to ask, but you and Roy do."

They turned from facing Steve and continued walking towards the hut, which had a vegetable garden on one side. On the other side, to Bill's disbelief, was a small bed of English flowers like the ones in his Mother's garden. Red met them outside and greeted each man with a simple word, "Welcome."

After the usual greetings Ian began the conversation by saying, "We stopped at a squatters hut north of here to ask directions to you, he directed us to here."

"That would've been my neighbour, was he young or old?"

"A young man with a rifle."

"That was Danny Grant, his dad Mick works for me, whenever he needs any money. Life is a bit like that around here, help is hard to find with everyone going to the goldfields."

They followed Red into his home of slab walls tightly installed together, creating a comfortable room. As they had noted from the outside, there were several rooms attached and it was bigger than it looked from the outside, surrounded by trees. It extended back into the undergrowth of the bush, giving the impression of a small hut. Red led them down a short hallway to a room overlooking a small garden, with cut grass and a bird bath in the middle of the grassed area. In a few moments they were joined by a woman wearing a veil over her face.

She walked forward saying, "Welcome to our home."

Red introduced his wife Mary to Bill and Ian, then turned to Steve and explained, "My dear this is Steve Baker, who is to go undercover with Roy."

She took Steve's hand and said, "I do hope you both will be safe, going after that man."

After speaking she retreated back into another room, behind a curtain.

"How are Fred and Roy progressing?" Ian enquired.

"Roy has taken a long time to learn to stay on his horse!" Red grinned and replied, before adding, "Fred's leg is improving, that bullet really did a lot of damage and the healing has taken a long time. He can stay on a horse for several hours at the present time, but not a full day's work."

"Have you heard from Sergeant Green?"

"I got a message to tell me that Fred is no longer required. I'm pleased because Fred will take a long time to be fit again."

"Bill and I are relieved to hear you say that he isn't well enough," Ian commented.

"Fred is to stay here until he's fit to return to duty" Red grinned.

Ian smiled and said, "We never thought you'd be a match for our Sergeant!"

Red laughed and gave an explanation, "We trained together a long time ago."

Red held up his hand which was a sign not to ask any more questions on this subject. He looked hard at Steve and asked, "Have you, like Roy, done prizefighting before joining the police?"

"Yes, two years of it."

"Good, that will be an advantage for you both, street fighters too?"

"Yes, that way we survived the hard times."

This was news to Ian and Bill, who looked at Steve in surprise. Steve saw the question in their eyes and said with a grin, "You didn't ask!"

"What else did you two do before joining the police?" Bill asked.

Again Steve smiled before speaking carefully, "This and that. We belonged to a street gang of like-minded boys who protected our street from those who demanded tokens of goodwill with menace. It was a rough area."

"Are you talking about fighting with no holds barred?" Ian enquired.

Steve's face hardened as he spoke, "Roy and I needed to survive the encounters with very dangerous men."

"And I thought I had a tough up bringing," Ian mused out loud.

Red spoke firmly, "Undercover work is cunning, you don't give quarter ever, you strike to survive. The man who wants to play the gentleman is doomed. This work is utterly ruthless, kill or be killed, that is the only way to survive this job."

Red's wife arrived with a tray of mugs of tea and they each took one and thanked her before she left the room. Red lit an oil lamp and placed it on the middle of the slab table. It was a massive construction surrounded by sliced logs, giving a flat surface for seats. All the furniture was made here, as required. The room had a scent of polished wood, using wax taken from the hives of wild bees.

"Bee stings don't cause me any problems," Red explained.

"We aren't good at climbing trees and bee stings are not agreeable to either of us. We make a point of never camping anywhere near them, but we do love the honey if it's ever available?" Bill said, glancing at Ian.

In the twilight the sound of approaching horses penetrated the room and instantly drew their attention. Red stood up and began to leave the room followed be the three men. Even though Roy and Fred were expected a group of horsemen could mean trouble until they had been identified correctly. Red walked across the open space between his home and the horse yards, followed by his visitors as Fred and Roy rode into the yard. They greeted Red as usual and Red moved aside stating the obvious, "We've got company!"

Roy alighted from his horse, saw Steve and greeted him with an affectionate hug. Bill and Ian looked surprised as they were unaccustomed to seeing men greet each other in this way. Red also saw their greeting but made no comment.

Steve saw their expressions and explained with a touch of hardness in his voice, "Roy is my brother and we always greet each other with a hug."

They accepted these two men as brothers. Red was able to take their greetings with each other a step further, now he had the proof that if one of them was in trouble, the other would, regardless of the situation, go to his aid. He'd been thinking that Roy ought to meet the twin girls who lived within riding distance of his place. Now he'd met Steve, they both ought to meet them, he thought and smiled to himself. In those few moments the men saw Red's smile and wondered what he was thinking, but no one was game enough to ask! After the greetings Fred and Roy unsaddled their horses and took them to the gate, took off their bridles and let them join the other horses in the paddock, then took their saddle bags to their hut. A water trough for the horses was outside the hut, and it was good enough for a wash to remove the dust of the day. A comb through the hair was enough to make themselves presentable, before walking back to where Red was talking to Bill, Ian and Steve.

Once they were together, Red led the men into his home to the main room with a long table. Red's wife Mary brought food into the room with Roy and Fred helping her. She seemed reluctant to sit with them, but Fred and Roy insisted and regardless of Red's comments made her sit down at the other end of the table facing Red.

"Mary, friends eat together," Fred said.

"If my wife wants to eat elsewhere, she can do as she wishes," Red said, obviously irritated.

"No Red, Mary eats with us or we'll leave now," Roy interjected firmly.

Red was unaccustomed to being challenged by young men and least of all in his own home. There was silence as everyone waited to hear what he'd say to Roy. He opened his mouth to speak and before Red could say a word, Roy stood up, went to Mary and gave her a hug.

"See, we want you to stay and we always get our way," Roy said.

Red had no choice but to grin, saving up words for later. He watched in surprise as Roy removed her veil.

"Mary, what's done can't be undone and we all love you, so what does it matter," Roy said.

In that moment Red felt a deep rush of affection for Roy as he saw the expression on his wife's face. There was his beloved Mary for the first time in years sitting at the table without her veil. No one at the table exhibited any surprise at the now visible scars on her face. Neither Ian, Bill nor Steve showed the shock they'd felt at seeing the veil removed and the scars revealed. Their expressions slowly changed to deep compassion. The meal progressed to mugs of tea which Fred left the room to procure from the kitchen shed separate to the hut. Mary was no fool and being sensitive had seen their shock, she also saw it change, to be replaced with an expression she would value for the remainder of her life.

"Red don't keep the boys up too late talking," Mary said, standing up when the meal was over.

"No dear I won't."

They smiled at one another as she passed through the curtain.

Red sighed and spoke quietly to Roy and Steve, "The training I'll give you will be hard, but it will be the best I can do. You know I was an undercover policeman in the city and I thought I was good at it. The man you are seeking didn't harm me, but he made me watch as he personally cut my Mary and she will carry those scars for life. I failed the one I love, and now you've been sent to me to train and I have to be tough with you." There was silence and he added, "If one of you is caught, the other will pay the price, do you understand?"

They looked at Fred and nodded and Red continued, "Many years ago I had a brother who used to make sweets and sell them to the children. I think he gave more away than he sold. He was a good man my brother, he refused to pay money to the man who cut Mary."

"What happened to him?" Bill asked.

"He was fed to the sharks alive as a warning, to other men watching it happen."

"When we were kids we were forced by his men to go to the wharf and watch him die," Roy said.

Red was visibly shocked as these words were being spoken by the two young men sitting at his table. He realized that they knew all about the man who had tortured his wife and that's why Roy knew Mary's veil wasn't the solution to her problem. Red also knew in his heart Roy was going nowhere near that man.

"I didn't know Roy, you didn't tell me when I asked if you knew anything about this man I'm going to train you to capture or kill," he said.

"Us kids loved the sweet seller and none of us played tricks on him. There were few people in our world who were kind to the street children," Steve said with his arm on Roy's shoulder.

"Red you cannot expect us to capture him, he is like a snake to be killed on sight," Roy said.

"Roy, you're a policeman and regardless of your private feelings, for either Mary or the seller of sweets, your job is to uphold the law," Ian spoke quietly.

"That man has lost any right to be protected by the law," Steve replied.

"Justice will come Steve, but not at your hand or Roy's either," Bill said gently.

Red moved suddenly and came and put his arms around Roy's and Steve's shoulders, giving them a gentle hug.

"I'd be jealous if Mary hugged you, so I'm doing it on her behalf, it's getting late," Red said.

"I'm going to my bed, you can talk until the moon rises, but I'm going now," Fred announced.

The others followed and Bill noticed Red had tears in his eyes as he turned to enter his home after seeing his friends out the door. It had been a difficult night for Red, bringing to mind the nightmare of being forced to watch the torture.

Chapter 5

The call to breakfast next morning came earlier than each man wanted to hear. None of them wanted to leave their swags as they heard the bell ringing for the second time. Bill and Ian washed in the trough, and Steve followed knowing Ian would say something if he didn't wash. Fred and Roy watched from a safe distance. Fred had a firsthand knowledge of Ian and washing and put a hand out to stop Roy walking into a sudden shower of water. Ian looked at Fred and Roy and pointed to the trough. Fred didn't move for a moment or two as he weighed up his options, deciding it would be a long day if he didn't comply, he took Roy's arm and walked to the trough.

"Must we?" Roy asked.

"Yes for peace if nothing else."

The five men presented themselves clean and tidy for the first meal of the day. Mary complimented them for washing out their sleep and looking fresh. Fred and Roy avoided looking at Ian, whom they saw had a smile on his face! On most days Fred and Roy had eaten in the kitchen shed well before sunrise. Red had also washed and now looked fresh for the day.

"The first job of the day for me is to test your riding ability Steve," he said.

Immediately after the meal they went to get the horses and were soon heard riding in a southerly direction. Bill and Ian walked over to a hut where Fred and Roy were checking their equipment.

Fred was replacing a leather strap on his bridle as Ian asked, "How's the leg?" "Almost healed now, only a slight twinge now and again."

"Heard from Jenny?" Bill enquired.

There was a sudden silence until Fred gave a reluctant answer.

"I haven't heard for some time. Now that I won't be going north we might be able to write directly to one another."

"Where will you be working from now?" Ian asked.

"I haven't been told yet."

"Now Steve is here you will be working together, how quick is Steve on the uptake?" Bill asked Roy.

"Steve is highly intelligent but doesn't show it. We've been in some tight places together and he can cope with anything," Roy replied cheerfully.

"Roy this is a very serious matter," Ian said sternly.

Roy grinned at Ian and replied, "When I said Steve and I have survived unpleasant encounters, I mean bad ones. We are quite capable of looking after ourselves, the proof is we are not dead yet!"

"Don't treat it lightly Roy," Ian said, clearly not satisfied.

"Ian, we survived living on the streets. We know how to live in bad places."

"Just remember there are others involved apart from yourselves."

"Ian don't worry, we know how to work in a group of people."

"Ian, I've worked with Roy, he's sharp in a corner, so don't worry," Fred added.

The men talked of other matters until they heard the approach of horses, looking down south saw Red riding beside Steve. Close at hand it was obvious that Red had had an enjoyable ride. He stopped beside Ian and said cheerfully, "He'll do."

Red rode to the horse yard and dismounted, unsaddling his horse and opening the gate into the horse paddock to let it go free. For a moment he watched this graceful animal gallop down to where the other horses were standing near some trees. Steve had also followed Red and the two men walked back to his hut. Mary had brought out mugs of tea and slices of freshly made damper.

"Are you satisfied with Steve?" She asked her husband.

Red looked at Steve and replied, "He's okay, he stayed on his saddle, when many men would have fallen off when I took him down to Hell's Corner."

"You took him down there! That's an awful ride."

"I told you Steve stayed on his horse."

"But Red, it's so dangerous."

Red grinned at his wife and explained, "Steve had no problem at all and his horse climbed out of it."

"Are you alright, not many men have come out of that place in one piece," Mary asked Steve.

"Roy warned me that Red would probably take me on that ride. He said to hang on to the horse and let it have its head and I'd be okay, so the horse and I became one!" Steve grinned and replied.

Red laughed along with everyone else and said, "He did too!"

"Which way did you climb out of it?" Roy asked.

"The steep way."

"That's almost impossible," Roy exclaimed in awe.

Red looking at Roy explained, "I didn't need to test you in this way, but I wanted to know what kind of man Steve was in a dangerous situation, and how he would be able to deal with it? Steve didn't show fear, not at all, I found out that his breaking point is beyond Hell's Corner."

"Roy and I have learnt not to show fear, even if we feel it. We discovered that to show fear is to admit defeat," Steve smiled at Red and told him.

"You did very well today and there are other ways to be tested, as you'll discover in the weeks ahead," Red said.

"Do you have a timeline in mind?" Bill asked.

"No, these boys won't be leaving here until I'm satisfied they can survive the work they have been chosen to complete."

"Please back up Red in your police discussions," Mary asked Bill.

"Of course both Ian and I will do as you request. We want to be able to see Steve and Roy when this job has been completed."

"I'm expecting Mick and Ken back today from taking a few head of cattle and delivering them to the new owners. Ken is also here being trained. Roy and Fred can tell you all about these men," Red informed the men.

Steve helped Roy complete his work with time to spare, so they walked down to the creek to talk and found an old log near the water. Now seated at either end of the wood, they needed a catch-up as the men had not seen each other for over six months.

"Are you still seeing Becky?" Roy asked Steve.

"No, she's gone off with another fellow."

"Who?"

"That bloke whose father owns the corner shop, two streets up from our place."

"I'd say good riddance, she's no good Steve."

"I thought we could've made a go of it."

"Not likely in the long term, you need someone who has more scope to her life."

"What have you in mind Roy?"

"I've met a pretty girl who has a twin sister."

"How long is it since you met this new girl?" Steve laughed and asked.

"I met her not long after I came here. Red asked me to go with him one day when he was taking a horse to a squatter a couple of miles from here."

Roy was speaking in a tone of voice which alerted Steve to the fact that this was serious. He didn't usually use this particular tone, when speaking about a female relationship.

"What's her name?" Steve asked carefully.

"Anne. She's beautiful, but I don't know what she thinks of me?'

This wasn't the Roy he'd always known, and Steve smiled and suggested, "Probably the same as you think of her."

"Do you think so Steve?"

"Yes why not, you're a handsome man as you well know Roy."

"I know I always get along well with girls, but this girl is different. I like her."

Treading carefully, Steve mused, "I don't think girls are different, some are brought up with manners. Some girls like the ones we have known in our street are no holds barred, as we both know Roy."

"Anne looks different."

Steve smiled at his friend and asked gently, "Have you seen Anne again since the first time?"

"Yes, I've seen her quite a few times. She comes up with her father to see Red, and I always seem to be nearby. I'm able to spend time with Anne while the two men talk."

Steve had never seen his friend go this deep and wondered if it was real, if so he'd give it his full support.

There was another matter which they needed to make a decision, it concerned their adopted Mother, if Roy stayed out here.

"Roy if you were to marry Anne, what do you intend to do about Mother?" Steve enquired.

"Probably time she retired."

"I think she's running a group now and enjoying it."

"I'd be reluctant to take her away from the life she enjoys in the city."

"Are the city police involved with her business, do you know?" Steve enquired.

"No, but I wouldn't be surprised if she had to pay someone."

"Roy, in coming out here you have to be respectable to marry Anne."

"We are respectable, sometimes!"

"But not our adopted Mother!"

"No Steve she's not in the least respectable, but she is Mother and will always be."

"How do you think she would like being out here?"

"Do you mean being a grandmother?"

They smiled at each other as they left the log and walked back up the hill.

"What's the name of the other twin?" Steve asked.

"Beautiful Betty, identical to my Anne, wait till you see them together, but remember hands off my Anne!!" Roy grinned at Steve and told him.

Steve gave Roy's shoulder a hug and replied, "I'll remember, sometimes!"

They walked around the side of the hut leading to the horse yards. The horses were standing in the shade of a couple of trees, suddenly they pricked up their ears and looked towards the east.

"Why are they doing that?" Steve asked.

Red, who was standing beside the yard, replied, "They know other horses are coming this way."

"How do they know?" Steve enquired

"I don't know, I'm not a horse!!" Red laughed.

Everyone laughed and Roy explained to Steve, "If you were to lay your head to the ground and press your ear to the soil, you can hear something coming faintly. Horses can identify themselves from these vibrations, and they move uneasily around the yard. They want to be free to run from danger."

"Do you believe it?" Steve looked at his friend and asked.

"That's what Fred told me," Roy said, adding quietly, "I tried it and heard the sound of cattle moving in my direction."

As they were talking the sound of the approaching horses became clearer. The horses in the yard settled down again as two horsemen rode into sight and up to where Red was standing, leaning against the fence. As they approached he straightened and walked a few steps forward to greet them. They were solid looking men, slim and strong. They dismounted and came towards Red, leading their horses. Neither man looked older than their late twenties.

"G'day Ken, Mick, have any trouble with the cattle?" Red spoke.

"No Red, all delivered safe and sound." Ken answered

"Good. Come and meet Roy's friend he's always talking about, and the other men."

"After we've seen to our horses," Mick replied.

"Come as soon as you're ready Mick"

Red smiled knowing the men would always put the welfare of their horses before their personal activities, after all it was what he demanded from his men.

He was aware of Steve's interest and Bill told him, "Steve is keen to learn and he soaks up knowledge."

"That's all very well, but he has so much to learn to give the impression that he has grown up on a farm," Red mused.

"I think he can do it after he learns the basics of the work."

"I hope you're right Bill."

Ken and Mick, after putting their hoses out in the paddock, came back to where Red was standing, and he introduced them to Steve. Their handshakes were firm and this was a good sign which was always noted by men meeting for the first time.

Red called out to Fred who had been helping in the horse yard, saying, "When you've finished go and put the cows in the yard and milk them, it will save Mary doing the job today."

Fred waved a hand cheerfully in the air as he turned to do this small job.

"I'm going to miss that boy when he returns to duty," Red said to Bill.

"Fred has obviously enjoyed being here for a good rest from police work," Bill responded.

Mick spoke before Red could say a word, "Rest you call it, why it's bloody hard work all the time!"

"But no one is trying to kill you while you are doing the work," Ken added.

Mick grinned and said, "That's a good point Ken, but it's still bloody hard work."

"You know these men have had an easy life here, they don't know what I've got up my sleeve for them yet!" Red explained to Bill.

"What is it Red?" Ken asked.

He grinned and clapped Ken on the shoulder and replied, "You'll find out all in good time."

Mary, who had come out of the hut to speak to Red, had remained quiet while he had spoken to Fred. Before anyone could question Red about the work he had in mind, she said, "What's that about you missing Fred, I'm the one who'll miss him. You've never milked a cow in your life!"

The men all grinned in obvious enjoyment at Red's discomfort and wisely remained silent as Red opened his mouth to speak. Mary put up her hand to silence him and continued, "I haven't finished yet. Fred has taught Roy to milk the cows. Now life will be a lot better until he has to leave here."

Red looked surprised and said, "So that's what Roy's been doing in the early mornings, when I've been trying to find him?"

"If you'd grown up on a farm Red, you'd know where to find men in the early mornings," Mary grinned at him and explained.

There was only so much Red could endure being the butt of their humour, and now he suggested, "Mary, what about some tea before the sun gets up any higher?"

She smiled and knowing the signs replied, "Yes dear!" then turned and retreated back into her hut.

Red expressed his feelings in a soft tone of voice, "Women!," to the grins of the men, as they silently followed him to the hut for the desired mugs of tea.

Steve followed Roy to the milking yard, who had explained, "I'll go and help Fred."

"Will you show me how to milk a cow?" Steve asked as he followed him.

"Yes, it's good for you to know, after all it's part of farm life."

"What else have you learnt to do here?" Steve enquired.

"How to stay alive!" Roy grinned.

"How different from what we've known is this life Roy?" Steve said.

Roy lent against the wooden fence and watched Fred encouraging the cows in a quiet voice to walk up to the yard.

"You remember how we, as young boys, had to learn the dangerous lanes and streets. We knew our area by studying all the pitfalls and safe houses. It was our landscape and we had to know it well to survive in that environment," he replied.

"Yes I remember and it was a painful learning experience."

"This life is really no different, the same types of men and women, people don't change that much anywhere. We just have to sort them out the way we did as boys.'

"What about here?"

"I've been too busy to make an assessment, gut feeling this is a safe place, in fact it feels like the home I've never enjoyed. Mary and Red are good people and Fred Hall is a mine of useful information."

Roy held the gate open and stood aside as Fred drove the cows into the yard shutting the gate when they were all inside the enclosure. Once Fred had chosen the first animal, Roy was ready with a rope halter and tied it to the fence, then Fred tied a back leg to the fence to stop the cow kicking over the bucket of milk. Taking it in turns the job was soon completed.

Fred had watched Steve making an effort to milk the last cow.

"I'd bet Steve, when you joined the police, you'd never thought milking a cow would be one of your duties," he laughed and said.

"Nothing shocks me anymore in this job, surprises yes."

"Really Steve?"

He was finding the job of milking difficult with Fred talking, now he had to answer, "Roy and myself saw a lot of nasty events when we were boys. So far the police have been tame in comparison, no doubt this will change in time."

"Watch it Steve, you just sprayed me with a squirt of milk," Fred exclaimed.

Steve looked up to see Fred wiping a spray of milk from his face and laughed and still grinning said, "So I did, you just had a drink!"

"I'll take over now Steve," Roy said, who was watching nearby.

He stood up from the stump and moved away to one side, as Roy completed the job. Fred and Roy each carried a bucket of milk up to Mary's hut. Red had made her a sheltered hut in which she could put the milk in pans to allow the cream to rise to the top, which would be skimmed off later.

Fred led the way to the long table in the shade of the trees outside Red's hut, where mugs of tea were waiting with fresh damper.

"What are you doing today?" Red asked Bill.

"Ian and I will be checking our equipment after going through the flooded creek."

"We're expecting a message from Sergeant Green," Ian added.

"No word has reached here yet."

"Are you waiting for a message too?" He turned to Fred and asked.

Red looked down the table and said cheerfully, "You boys will be here for some weeks, so settle down and enjoy Mary's cooking."

"And Red's hard work!" Ken added.

There was general laughter as they began to walk away to do the various jobs.

"The man who works my horses, Ben, knew you a long time ago," Red said to Bill.

"Did he say where?"

"No, but you'll find him in the hut near the horses."

Bill took Ian's arm saying, "Come on, we'll investigate."

Ken talked to Roy about the troughs needing more water and Steve was roped into this job too. They collected their buckets and walked down to the creek. On the way down the track they passed Ben's hut, where his wife and children were living. Outside there was a tent and Roy told Steve, "Ben won't sleep in an enclosed room with his family. Something happened to him in the city a long time ago. Even in really cold weather he stays outside in his tent."

Steve had listened and now remembered Bill's story of the brick kiln, which he now told to the men.

"We heard Red mention Ben to Bill, perhaps that's the connection?" Ken suggested.

"Nothing remains secret forever, small pieces of information come together to make a truth or at least explain an event," Roy mused.

"That's our job to gather information," Ken added.

"You're a policeman?" Steve asked in a sudden realization.

"Yes I am, and like you, we're being trained to be stockmen."

"We, meaning Mick too?" Steve enquired.

"No, He's training me."

Roy stopped walking in shock. He'd been working with Ken for two months and he had never revealed in any way that he was a policeman. He didn't know exactly what he felt about this revelation. Steve saw Roy's face begin to show anger. Ken was also watching Roy's expression change.

Roy asked him, "Why didn't you tell me?"

"You didn't need to know at the time, Roy."

"What caused the change?"

Ken looked at Steve and replied, "Steve has arrived and I think that he has a way of knowing other people's secrets."

"He does, does he?"

"There's no point in getting angry Roy, it never solves any problems," Ken grinned and said.

Ken was watching Roy carefully and was almost sure he knew what was coming next and wondered how he could avoid it. In a split-second Steve drew his attention from Roy who saw an opportunity and threw half a bucket of water at Ken. Ken had excellent reflexes and managed to get only partly wet.

He laughed, not in the least offended, and said, "You missed!"

"You deserved a good drenching, Ken"

"I know Roy, but it was a police order to remain secret."

"Mick is training you for what job?"

"I don't know yet."

"Secrets everywhere!" Steve laughed and said.

They carried buckets of water up from the creek making a number of trips to fill the horses troughs.

"So this is why habitations are close to water," Steve commented.

"Water is the life blood of man and beast. Sometimes in Summer these little creeks dry up and water has to be carried for quite a distance," Ken explained.

"What would Red have said if he'd seen Roy toss that water at you?"

Ken glanced at Roy and answered, "Down by the creek, probably nothing, anywhere else and you'd be carrying buckets all day."

Roy wasn't happy at being at a disadvantage and grumbled, "I still don't know why you had to keep it a secret, as you were one of us."

Chapter 6

At the long table Red was speaking to Mick about the next job to be done the following Day. He looked as Roy, Steve and Ken approached him.

"Ken, I'm sending you into the ranges with Mick to muster a herd of cattle. I want you to bring them back down the spur to the creek below the huts," he said.

"Do you know how many there are in the herd?" Mick asked Red.

"No. I haven't done a full muster for a couple of years, there's a bull with them, so the number could be high."

"Where do you think we'll need to look for them?' Ken enquired.

"The best grass is in the areas near water, I'd doubt they'd walk up the barren hills, unless something chased them in that direction."

"Ken and I will enter at the top end, a mile or so north of here and work our way down in this direction," Mick suggested.

Red agreed with this idea and the two men went away to prepare their equipment ready for an early ride the next morning.

Red turned to Roy and Steve saying, "I'm sending you both into the ranges to continue the muster from the southern end. You'll ride down the creek just above the entrance to 'River Oaks.' You can also leave in the early morning. Alan Gill is highly knowledgeable about the area you'll be riding, so listen to him."

The men left to check their equipment and collect their rations. Mary had reminded Roy that they may have to live off the land and to take extra bullets.

Ian, who had listened to the instructions, waited until the men were out of hearing range and said to Red, "Bill and I know from experience that there are lawless men in those ranges. Roaming stock means food for men on the run or just living rough in the isolated valleys."

Red grinned and after a moment said quietly, "We've heard how those two men have endured hard times, this is another test."

Bill began to speak, but Red raised his hand and interrupted.

"Bill, Ian, I know what I'm doing, leave it with me. What was in the note you have just received from Sergeant Green?"

"Bill and I are to leave in the morning to scout a distant gold field where a problem has been reported. He also has written that the Alex Hunt Carriers have been sent here, to collect Steve's Police saddle and equipment, plus his horse."

"Who are these carriers?'

"We met them last summer, a good family. You'll like Tom and Dick and they'll have a couple of other men with them for security," Ian explained.

"Fred?"

"Sergeant Green wants him to take a message to Sam Hade, his wife is the Sergeant's sister, Elizabeth. Jenny their daughter and Fred wants to become engaged," Bill smiled and replied.

"He's not having an easy time from what little I've heard Fred speaking about his friend," Red mused.

"No, Jenny's Mother isn't keen on her becoming engaged to a policeman."

They talked for a little while before both Ian and Bill went away to prepare for their departure the next morning. Fred was visibly excited to be going to the Wade farm.

That night Mary commented on losing all her boys and asked Red, "Who is going to do the milking?"

" A lovely lady called Mary is going to do the milking!!" he replied.

"That is what I thought Red would say!"

The boys cheerfully made all the proper replies and the evening passed quickly.

In the early morning as the stars faded, just after dawn Mary heard the sound of the horses hooves passing her hut. Almost an hour later the sound of two more riders passing, 'that will be Roy and Steve' she thought, going south.

Mary was quite correct. Roy had said to Steve just after dawn when he had woken up, hearing the other men leaving.

"Steve we have a short way to ride to 'River Oaks'. We can leave later, after all we don't want to arrive before they have breakfast."

They talked as they rode south with tall hills east of their horses, in the west open plains. Even though there was no need to hurry, Steve noticed Roy didn't let his horse break from a brisk pace. He smiled and kept his horse alongside Roy. 'River Oaks' was situated on a rise above a creek, which flowed between the tall hills. It was above flood level, which meant water had to be carried a reasonable distance to the house. Steve found himself looking at country dwellings with new eyes. This one as it came into sight was a combination of stone and wooden slabs. The stone section had shingles on the roof and was at the front of the house. Roy led the way to the back of the house after explaining.

"The hitching rail under that tree is for visitors, I always ride around to the horse yard, where I can unsaddle my horse."

Steve smiled to himself and followed Roy into an area surrounded by trees. As they dismounted two men came out of the nearest slab hut.

Roy spoke quietly, "The older man is Mr. Gill and his son Victor."

After tying up their horses to a rail under a tree, they walked forward with Roy in front greeting them, before standing aside and saying, "This is my friend Steve Baker."

Each man sized up the other one as they greeted each other, the overall impression being one of satisfaction. Victor was tall like his Father, both well-built and tanned from long days in the sun. Their handshake was equally firm and the smiles of welcome to Roy and Steve were genuine. Steve instantly liked the men and more so when he heard, Mr. Gill say, "Now you're here Roy I won't get any work out of my daughter Anne!"

Steve was amused to see Roy blush, as he heard him say, "Whatever gave you that idea?"

Mr. Gill laughed and Victor said, "Steve I don't think Roy knows which of my twin sisters is Anne!"

Roy heard and corrected him, "You're wrong Victor, I know which is Anne."

"I don't know why you're so sure, she's my own sister and I'm never sure which is which," Victor said

Roy grinned at him, holding his secret in his heart.

Steve followed Mr. Gill into a large room with a long table, like the one in Red's house. An older woman stood up to greet him, with Mr. Gill saying, "Steve Baker, my wife Eva."

Steve greeted Mrs. Gill and turned slightly as he heard footsteps enter the room. There was a sudden silence as Victor introduced his sisters, watching Steve's face as he did so with obvious humour. The family seemed to enjoy these introductions, because Steve was aware of their smiles as he looked at the beautiful girls. Both had done their hair the same way, the same light blue blouse buttoned to the neck, pale dresses to the ankles and sensible black shoes. All identical. Roy stepped forward and greeted Anne to the surprise of her entire family.

"How can you tell Roy?" Victor asked

Roy smiled and remained silent for a moment, "It's a secret Victor."

In the general laughter which followed Steve gazed at Betty and thought he'd never seen such a beautiful girl in all his life. She had lovely brown hair which caressed her shoulders. Now he saw a lovely smile as she became aware of his interest and he blushed slightly as he remembered to breathe! Betty was equally aware of this attractive man looking at her.

She stepped forward holding out her hand, saying, "I'm Betty Mr. Baker."

To which he replied, "I'm called Steve…."

Across the room Eva Gill smiled looking at her daughter Betty and her husband saw her expression and asked quietly, "What's on your mind?"

"The cows have to be milked," She smiled and replied.

Victor heard the word 'cows' and took the hint, saying, "Come on Betty, milking time."

Reluctantly Betty stepped away from Steve and followed her brother out of the room, watched by Steve, thinking how graceful she moved, like a swan.

"After you've had a mug of tea and something to eat, we'll talk about the mustering job," Mr. Gill said to Roy.

There was no doubt that Roy and Anne were close friends, as Mrs. Gill expressed her thoughts to her daughter, "Anne, concentrate on your work, forget about Roy, or we'll never get lunch started!"

"But Mum, he's hardly ever here," Steve heard Anne say.

"Anne dear, Roy haunts the place as you well know.!"

"Now he's going away again."

"That's the way of men, dear."

Their voices faded out of Steve's hearing as they closed the door and went to another part of the house. Steve had watched Anne leave, thinking about her lovely sister Betty. Looking across the room he saw Mr. Gill looking at him with a smile. Steve felt himself blushing ever so slightly, as the older man said, "My daughters always create discomfort to our visitors. They love to dress in identical clothes and play! Roy always knows Anne from the very first meeting, which is a mystery to all of us."

"Roy has a unique way of knowing all kinds of things, including things I'd rather he didn't know. He will always know Anne."

"You and Roy are close friends?" Mr. Gill enquired.

"Yes, we're like brothers and have been since we were young children. At the same time we're individuals and close friends."

They talked on other subjects and later he saw a smile on Mr. Gill's face and wondered what he was thinking.

In the late morning Mr. Gill talked about the ranges and the art of mustering semi-wild cattle saying, "I'd be surprised if you find more than twenty to forty head, some would have been slaughtered for food by starving men and some may have died natural deaths. Try and keep away from other men if you can, to avoid trouble. Don't take risks unnecessarily."

After lunch Betty took Steve to muster horses from a paddock below the house. He spent a happy afternoon in her company, doing one job after another. They discovered a similar sense of humour and enjoyed laughing together. Betty was an excellent horsewoman and Steve learnt a few more things about the nature of riding a horse. She was a good teacher and these ideas would prove useful in the months ahead in summer. In the evening Roy and Steve fitted into the circle of this happy family as if they'd been there forever. For Roy and Steve they'd never been part of a close-knit family, and it was a unique experience, particularly for Steve. He now knew and understood the change he'd seen in Roy. Next morning Steve and Roy left 'River Oaks' at sunrise and followed the creek into the ranges.

Chapter 7

Mr. Gill wasn't the only one who watched them leave, he'd liked Steve and wanted to see him again, at the same time knowing in part what was in store for that young man. He sighed, thinking he had one of them at least, Roy and Anne. His son was bringing a horse up from the paddock as he watched the men depart. Now giving his attention to Victor, who after securing the reins began to look at each of the iron horseshoes, checking that they were firmly attached to the hooves. His father sat on a stump and watched him.

"When do you want me to leave?" Victor asked.

"About midday and make sure you're never seen by anyone."

"I will Dad, I've done it before when needed."

"Be very careful Victor."

"I will Dad, don't worry.'

"I do worry because you're my son."

It was a subdued meal with the family, and Victor left his home and rode down the creek and into the ranges. For the first two days it was an easy way of keeping well out of sight. Roaming the tops of the high hills and looking down into the dark valley floors, watching all movement. Victor enjoyed this kind of work, it was a lot better than gathering stones to build walls. Here it was a challenge of bushcraft. He thought about the care he had to take, like now making his evening fire in a pit where it couldn't be seen, behind the rocks. He finished his meal and was sitting quietly daydreaming, when he was suddenly in deep shock, almost paralyzed as he felt an iron hand around his neck. and heard

"Not one move or you will never breathe again, who are you?" He heard.

"Your future brother-in-law!" Victor croaked out.

The merciless hold weakened and Victor slowly turned around to face Steve, who asked, "Why?"

"To keep you safe from the outlaws in these hills."

A cold chill went down Steve's spine as he spoke quietly, "Victor, you were very close to dying. I'm good with knives, but I wanted to know things so you're still alive."

"Where's Roy?"

"Asleep."

Victor asked carefully of this suddenly very dangerous man, "What do you want to know?"

Steve saw his fear and leaning back against a stone spoke quietly. They talked and Victor relaxed. Steve told him that it wasn't a good idea to shadow men, unless it was his job, they talked until Steve asked, "When you next see your father, tell him please, that I don't want Roy to go north with me."

"You don't have to worry about that idea, he will be staying here with us eventually, I heard Dad talking to Red, not close enough to hear everything."

Steve laughed quietly, stood up and said, "I'd better be getting back to my camp."

Victor had also stood up and he was both surprised and gratified when Steve unexpectedly gave him a hug and whispered, "One day I hope you are my brother-in-law."

In the next instant he'd gone as silently as he had arrived, not a sound. It was sometime before Victor could close his eyes, he could still feel that hand around his throat. What was really disturbing to Victor was that a city man could move so quietly in the bush without being heard by him. It took some time for sleep to come.

Chapter 8

It was almost nine days later when Ben called out to Red, "Boss there's a mob of cattle coming down the spur of the creek."

They'd been preparing an area for the cattle in a flat space below the huts, now the cattle were to it. Being semi-wild Ben wasn't sure they'd stay, so he was surprised that they seemed contented. There were cows and calves which Red divided and took to another place along with the bull. The others were earmarked for a southern saleyard. No time was lost, Red had employed two other men who had been robbed on the gold field and wanted another life. They owned a dray and two horses and they were camping near the creek when the cattle arrived.

"You and Mick will join the other men to take these cattle down to the southern saleyards," Red explained to Roy.

"What is Steve doing?" Roy asked.

"He'll be doing another job with Ken."

It was obvious that Roy didn't like the idea of being separated from his friend for a long period of time while he was away with the cattle. Later in the evening Red had a quiet word with Steve, who in turn had a talk with Roy. He explained the importance of the droving experience, while he was doing another job.

In the early morning the men had the cattle moving before the sunrise, Mick and the two other men, kept the animals from straying out of the herd.

Steve gave Roy a big hug and Roy whispered into his ear, "I know."

Steve tightened his hug, and replied, "I want you safe."

"When will I see you again?"

"I'll return to "River Oaks" and see if Betty will have me?"

"I'll guard her for you!"

 Poor Betty, was Steve's thought.

They parted and neither looked back at the other, as Roy mounted his horse and rode after the herd as it left Red's place. Red noticed that Steve's face had turned pale and he gently put his arm around Steve's shoulder, in an unusual display of emotion.

"Roy will be okay and so will you, so don't worry Steve," he said.

Red dropped his arm as Steve spoke, "Thanks."

They stood watching until the dust had settled after the departed cattle had disappeared through the trees.

"What are we doing now?" Steve asked.

Ken, who had walked up to where Red and Steve were standing, heard Red's reply.

"You and Ken are to go north, after the carrier brings your saddles, swags and horses."

Red took a paper out of his pocket and handed it to Ken, saying, "Read it yourselves."

Steve leaned over Ken's shoulder and read Sergeant Green's note, which was quite detailed in content.

Ken looked up at Red saying, "Special saddles, all of our equipment to be well-worn and our clothes to be shabby. Nothing personal at all."

"Ken, from the moment you and Steve leave here, you must act the part of out of work stockman. If you meet police, act like stockmen, be surly and difficult, never ever let on you are other than what you appear to be. One other detail, when the carrier comes, keep out of sight," Red added.

With these instructions in their minds, Steve and Ken walked across the yard to the hut they were sharing.

Ken spoke quietly, "We'll have to wait and see what has been sent down to us to use on this assignment. I'd expect our swags, with our personal property will go back to the police barracks at Hill Top.'

"I expect so."

Each man began to think about the coming assignment. In the late afternoon the carrier arrived and the men watched from their hut, as two horses were being put in the yard.

"Steve, those are poor horses, look at them." Ken expressed in dismay.

"I am Ken, we have a long ride ahead of us, and it will seem like forever!"

Ken laughed and said, "You're not wrong, look at those saddles!"

"We really will be poor stockmen."

In those few minutes, of seeing the horses and saddles, the reality of the coming job dawned upon them, for the first time in a couple of years, they'd be on their own, without the protection of the law. They would be on the other side of the law. This realization was for a few moments quite daunting.

"Ken we are police, we are to do a job, we are colleagues and I believe we will succeed in this job," Steve said

Ken looked at Steve and added

"We've been given very poor equipment which places us at a disadvantage, couldn't we have had better horses?"

"How long do you think we could keep them as poor stockmen?"

Ken laughed. "One day, before someone would accuse us of stealing them!!"

"Cheer up Ken, treat it like an adventure!"

Hearing approaching footsteps they moved back into the hut, as Red entered carrying two swags.

"Change into your act, I will bring your boots and a coat each in a minute," Red said.

They talked to one another as they stripped out of their better-quality clothes and put on the shabby ones, which were none too clean. They looked at each other and laughed,

"I wouldn't trust you with a shilling!" Ken said.

Steve grinned, "I'd lock you up at the first opportunity!"

In no time their own swags were packed with all their property, including their long black boots.

Red came and made the collection saying, "Don't trim your beards and keep away from girls who ply the trade."

Chapter 9

In the early morning Steve and Ken rode away from Red Bryant's comfortable and safe property into their unknown new world. Red had watched these brave men leave, with the hope they'd be safe. The carrier left the next day for Hill Top with the three police horses and equipment.

Steve and Ken rode at a steady pace, neither man wanted to stop until they were a good distance from Red's place. By mid-afternoon the ranges were just visible on the eastern horizon.

"An early camp do you think?" Ken suggested.

"Yes, you choose."

They rode for another hour before Ken chose a place beside a creek on an open area with scenic views in all directions. Both men hadn't examined their new swags or the contents.

Mary had also given each of them a bag of rations saying, "Red told me to be careful."

She'd smiled at Ken and Steve and continued, "For your first night, finish the treats."

They'd thanked Mary and now after a long day in the saddle were curious to see what was in the bags.

The horses had to be hobbled and Ken enquired, "Do you think these hobbles are strong enough to hold the horses?"

Steve knelt down and looked carefully at them and said, "They're worn out." Standing up again he continued, "We'll need to do some work on them to make them stronger."

"Why do you think they gave us such poor equipment?" Ken asked.

"Perhaps because they don't expect to see it again."

"That's what I've been thinking."

Ken mused as he picked up the two-quart pots and walked down to the creek to fill them up. Returning he picked up his swag where he had left it beside his saddle and took it to the other side of the fire, out about ten feet opposite to where Steve had placed his swag. If anyone came when they were asleep, it was a safe position. Opening their swags they were gratified to find sewing leather material and other bits and pieces, apart from a change of clothes full of patches.

Ken had spread the contents out on the grass and looked up at Steve saying, "We have been well supplied and can mend our own equipment, if we get separated."

"I hope we never get separated, in fact we must do our level best to stay close like glue," Steve said.

"Did you see that rider who rode out of Red's place late last night?" Ken asked, changing the subject.

"No I didn't, who was it?"

"I don't know, I asked Red and I thought he looked uncomfortable."

"Did he answer you?"

"Not really, which it is why it stuck in my mind."

Steve sat quietly looking into the flames not seeing all the colours in the fire, and spoke, "How much information do you think has been kept from us?"

"I don't know Steve, my gut feeling is that it has been planned carefully to get us into the valley without being shot."

Steve stirred the fire with a stick, sending up a shower of sparks which vanished in to the night and mused, "I think you're right and I wonder what we'll face on this ride north."

Ken removed a slab of meat from his bag. This was the treat and Steve found one too.

"This meat could get us into a lot of trouble in our changed circumstances."

They also discovered fresh damper and honey.

"Red won't be happy when he discovers that Mary has given away his supply of wild honey!" Ken laughed and said.

They raised their mugs of tea to Mary Bryant. It had been a long day, with a good meal and all the meat consumed, they put the fire out and went to their swags for an early night.

As usual the two policemen left camp at sunrise, continued at a slow pace in a northerly direction, sometimes talking and as customary, long hours in silence, each man in his own daydream. Some of these areas between the hills were a few miles from rise to rise. Frequently on these long stretches there were no water courses, and if any were seen they'd dry up in the hot months, which was why Ken and Steve rode close to the hills keeping a good distance from the gold fields and staying away from the traffic of miners walking from one field to another.

The next three days were uneventful, no one bothered them and it was easy riding.

"My horse is probably walking at two miles an hour, if that," Ken complained

"Mine too. I wonder where Sergeant Green found them."

"I wonder if he intentionally chose slow horses."

"Even out of work stockman have better horses and equipment, from what I've seen this side of the mountains," Steve replied.

"So why have we been given such bad horses and equipment?"

"What else was in that note Red gave us to read?" Steve asked.

Ken stopped riding and let his horse nibble at a patch of green grass, his colleague did likewise and Ken answered, "I'd forgotten about that note, it seemed to have been put in as an afterthought, strange really."

"What was written at the bottom of the page?"

"That on our ride north, we would be contacted by a policeman, dressed like ourselves, he would give us instructions."

Steve was silent as he digested the new information, before saying, "Ken, how do they know where we are in this vast open country?"

"To answer that question, we'd need Roy, he'd know the answer!"

"He would too, Roy always knows secrets."

Ken turned in his saddle and looked at Steve saying, "Do you really think you can keep Roy away from this job if we get into a major problem?"

"He's safe on that cattle drive for some weeks. Later he's to return to "River Oaks" and Anne will keep him occupied."

"You're kidding yourself Steve. I haven't worked all those weeks with Roy, without getting to know him well. In his feelings he has immense strength and nothing will bar his way if he wants to go somewhere. You know it too." Ken laughed and said cheerfully.

"How do you know?"

There was a slight touch in Steve's voice, like a brother's enquiry, which Ken recognized and didn't take offence to, before he began to speak.

"One of our jobs was mustering cattle in a valley on the edge of the ranges. I was bucked off my horse and landed badly. Roy found my horse and came looking for me. I've never known how he found me in a dry gully with steep sides. He managed to get me up on to his horse and walked back to our camp leading it. Mick was able to fix me up in a couple of minutes of sheer pain putting my shoulder back in place."

The horses finished eating and began to walk forward, as Steve voiced his thoughts about Roy, "That's Roy at his best. I've never known where this gift comes from, could be his mother's line from overseas."

"If Roy wants to come he will."

"Anne has a strong pull on him."

"So do you Steve, and if it's a choice between you and Anne, I'd put a couple of shillings on you winning!"

"Let's forget about Roy."

Ken was wise enough to let the matter drop. He continued to think about him for the remainder of the day, as a new friend. He wondered how Roy was getting on with the cattle drive.

They camped beside another creek, probably not far from a gold field. Ken drew Steve's attention to the plumes of blue smoke rising in the east beyond some hills. Steve strengthened the hobbles before putting them on the horses again, these seemed to be regular jobs, while Ken mended a leather strap on his bridle.

There was no one in sight as the moon rose and began to cast shadows around the camp. They were quite happy to remain silent during the meal, as their rations were now on the low side. Ken began to notice that Steve was staring into the bush behind him. He indicated that Ken was to remain seated. Suddenly Steve stood up and threw his knife, Ken turned to see a white face at the edge of their camp.

The man was close enough to the edge of the camp to hear a whizz beside his ear and see a knife sticking out from a sapling inches from where he was standing. In total shock he stopped walking and heard a cold voice say, "Drop any weapons and walk carefully forward, make no sudden movement or you will die."

The man walked forward slowly and trembling in shock, with his eyes on the two men, both standing and armed.

"I'm a friend," He said with a tremor in his voice.

He watched as Ken put down his rifle and Steve put another knife back in its pouch. In those brief moments the man felt a cold shiver down his spine, he'd been warned to be careful, but he didn't expect a man with a knife.

"I'm a policeman," he said quietly.

He was able to prove his identity to Steve's and Ken's satisfaction with relief saying, "My name is Tony Bane and my barracks is at Green Hills, my Sergeant's name is Ray Shaw. I have a message for you."

In the fire light Tony was dressed in shabby old stockman's clothes, even so nothing could hide the fact of his strength in arms and legs. Slim and eagle eyed, Steve thought. His movement was slow and controlled, as he sat down on the creek side of their fire. Moonlight cast long shadows and he had felt safe, as he had approached this camp, this was the first time he'd been caught.

"Tony why at night and not in the day?" Ken asked, as Steve went to retrieve his knife.

"Too many eyes in daylight."

"We haven't seen anyone of note."

"Ken you've been seen by a number of people. Stockmen like you two and the way you are dressed give the impression of being dangerous. People keep their distance from you."

"Dangerous?" Steve enquired.

Tony grinned, "You must know you're riding towards an area which is known to have a large number of lawless men roaming the hills."

Ken remained silent and Tony continued, "That's why you're dressed in the way you are now, as I am. No questions are asked and I can move without comment."

"What does the good Sergeant Green have to say?" Steve asked.

"I'm carrying a verbal message from him."

"Have you eaten tonight?" Ken asked.

"No. I left my horse back there," Tony pointed with his hand and continued, "I do have some food with me."

"Go and get it," Steve said briskly.

Tony slipped quietly back into the shadows, they heard his first few footsteps and then a silence.

"He does move quietly, I didn't hear him until you moved and the knife flew over my head!" Ken spoke quietly.

"I saw his shadow as he crossed a small slice of moonlight."

"I wonder if he knows how close he came to death this night?' Ken voiced.

Ken was wrong about it. Tony reached his horse and pressed his face into the horses neck and expressed to his mare, "I nearly met my Maker tonight, they should 've warned me that he threw knives and asked questions later."

Tony stood for a few moments with his arms around the horse's neck with his head buried in in her comforting mane. At last he sighed, unhitched the bridle and walked back to the camp and tied her up to a tree.

"I have meat for my meal. I brought extra for you as I'd been told you may be low in supplies," he said.

"They are low, thanks," Ken replied.

Steve now relaxed added, "We've been talking about getting some meat and if you'd been an enemy, we'd have plenty!"

Tony shivered and said, "I wasn't told about your ability with knives or I would've been a lot more careful"

"Never mind, what's the message?" Steve replied.

"A plan has been formulated which, if it works out properly, you'll be taken into the hills by lawless men. The police hope you'll be taken into a valley which is heavily guarded. We don't know exactly what's in this valley as no police have survived penetration. You are not to ask questions, that will get you killed, just observe everything. Make no notes and don't look as if you are observing anything."

"How do we get out?" Steve asked.

"The Sergeant expects you will be in the valley for a couple of months before it will be possible to find a way out on foot. If you're caught you'll be killed. He suggests you train your bodies to do without constant food."

"Is there anything the Sergeant really wants to know about in the valley?" Ken asked.

"Yes. We want to know what track they exit the valley with a dray and where the main group of huts are situated. There is something happening in the valley apart from the belief of an activity which the government agents are interested in closing down."

"Is this our final instructions from our Sergeant?' Steve asked.

"Yes, that's correct Steve."

The meal was cooked and eaten, during this time Tony passed on police news and told some funny stories. It was soon obvious that Tony wanted to leave, as he stood up and walked to his horse,

"Have we been shadowed?" Steve asked quietly.

Tony wasn't able to hide the expression which flashed across his face, as he replied,

"No, not to my knowledge."

He continued walking to his horse and they listened to him riding away into the night.

"They had to know where we were camped to send Tony Bane." Steve said as he put out the fire.

Ken stood looking down into the dying coals of the fire and said, "I wonder what we will experience next on this ride?"

"We'll find out soon enough Ken, sleep well."

Chapter 10

The next day they continued riding north and Ken commented, "I didn't know you carried knives Steve."

"I keep them hidden on my person, it's safer if no one knows. I never know when I might need them."

"Keep it secret where we are going."

"You can't see them now, can you? Warn me if ever you do see them Ken, as they may well save our lives."

"No I can't see them. I'm happier using my fists as I learnt to do in the streets as a kid, staying with my Granny in the city."

"Same here and I lived in the city in the Rocks area, it's amazing what you can do with fists and knees in a street fight!!"

They talked as they rode north, keeping a wary eye out for strangers and groups of men coming in their direction.

"Ken, I think we have company up ahead," Steve said quietly as they crossed a hill and rode into a wooded area.

"Who?"

"From this distance, I think they are police and we have to avoid being stopped and questioned by them."

"Do you think they've seen us?"

"I don't know Ken."

They had stopped riding and were secluded amongst the trees, a little to the west of where their horses were standing was a deep gully.

"We could avoid them by using that gully," Ken suggested.

Steve sat quietly on his horse looking in the distance at the police and after a few moments replied, "If we meet police, it's best to be out in the open, where we won't be hidden from other eyes. Your suggestion is the way we'll go, laying low on our horse's neck."

Ken turned his horse and followed an animal track which led down into the side of the gully. He was relieved to see it was free of water.

"Ken you lead and we'll move quickly. We need to get as far away as we can from the police."

Lying low the horses had no problems moving at a brisk pace down the surface of this split in the earth. They were fortunate that in some places the water had dug out deep holes, leaving flat areas near them which were easily passed.

"There are frequently more animal tracks leading out of this gully in this area. I want to see if we are on our own again," Ken said after about ten minutes.

Steve rode up beside his horse and took Ken's bridle as he left his saddle and began to climb up an animal track. Slowly he raised his head above the edge of the gully and looked in all directions. Looking back along the top of the gully, something caught his eye, a movement, as yet unidentified.

"I think we're under observation," he said, looking down at Steve.

"Are they police?"

"I don't think so, they're aware of us in the gully and they could be wary of the police too." Ken took his bridle from Steve and mounted his horse. "They're on the other side of the gully from where we saw the police."

"We can forget about them and continue down this gully."

They rode along the dry water bed until the sides became less steep, before turning a sharp bend and ending in a creek, which suited them both as it was good cover.

"How far away do you think is the settlement called Green Hills?" Ken asked as they headed north again.

"I don't know, but if those police were from Green Hills, it can't be far away."

"How do you make that out?"

"I didn't see a packhorse, did you?"

"No, they didn't have one."

"With that number of men, if they'd been travelling a long distance they'd almost certainly have a pack horse. You know that as well as I do," Steve explained.

Ken fell silent for a few minutes and spoke quietly, "We'll have to be able to assess situations and get it right the first time, if we want to survive this job."

Steve grinned at Ken and said, "Fortunately for us the men we'll encounter won't be rich enough to have a pack horse!"

They talked as they rode down the valley keeping close to the trees, constantly keeping their eyes peeled for any sign of the police.

"I think the police are stopping out of work stockmen from riding into the northern country at the present time, which is out of their control." Steve mused.

Ken interrupted Steve as he began to continue, "You're forgetting this is a free country and we can go anywhere providing we obey the law."

"Or how police interpret the law," Steve added.

"Which is frequently unjust, depending upon how that policeman is feeling at the time, and you know that as well as I do Steve."

"Which is why we're avoiding an encounter with the police, if we can get around them on our way north."

"I don't intend to be arrested for riding north," Ken added.

Steve was firmly of the same opinion saying, "We'll act as out of work stockmen and fight if we have to protect ourselves."

The creek turned in a westly direction and reluctantly they left it's shady trees and crossed the valley, and up to the crest of the hill and rested the horses amongst a patch of trees.

"What do you see?" Steve asked.

"I'd like to stay here for a little while and keep looking in that valley, I can't see any movement of men. They ought to be in sight and our horses aren't good enough to outrun a major confrontation."

"Alright but we can't stay long up here. We need to find a camp."

The longer they stayed the more concerned Ken became because he couldn't see any sign of men or horses. He knew they were out there somewhere beyond his excellent eyesight. A hour later they rode north and continued looking out for any movement. Both men were on edge and wanted to avoid trouble. In the late afternoon Steve chose a camp site in a long valley. It wasn't ideal being so open, but it had good grass and water for the horses and some high rocks near the creek edge.

Ken looking at the site suggested, "We normally put our swags opposite, but not tonight, if we have to fire our guns one of us might get shot."

"Good point, we'll camp with our backs to those rocks and make our fire about ten feet in front of us," Steve agreed.

"You do that while I find some branches with dead leaves to put behind the rocks, so no one can creep up in that direction."

Steve could hear Ken moving branches and smiled, they were learning aspects of survival and how to avoid problems with other men who might want to impede their journey. They had decided they'd lost their shadow-rider and felt a welcome freedom. Keeping this freedom was the upmost challenge in their minds, as each man went about preparing for the night. Steve had killed a young kangaroo a couple of days ago, and the last of this meat was cooking on the fire.

Waiting for the meat to be ready to eat, they enjoyed a mug of tea, when suddenly Ken whispered, "I can hear men approaching, more than three men with horses."

"Perhaps they're the men we saw earlier today and the scent of the cooking meat brought them to our camp."

"We can't afford to draw attention to ourselves, so no guns," Ken whispered before adding, "Or knives!"

Steve grinned at him and spoke, "At least knives are quiet."

"Until they hit their target!"

Steve asked, "What do you want to do now?"

"There are too many of them for us to stay here, we can't fight them all and win. We'll have to leave our meat cooking and creep away into the night."

Steve saddled the horses, while Ken packed up their camp, silently and quickly, handing Steve his unwrapped swag, they mounted and rode away in the moonlight. Looking back Ken glimpsed in a patch of moonlight four men leading horses, stumbling over logs close to their camp.

"I'd like to defend our camp."

"We can't afford to draw attention to ourselves, nor can we afford to lose our horses."

Ken wasn't in the least happy and expressed, "I'm never going to forget not defending our camp against men coming to steal our food."

"What do you think I'm feeling too?"

"The same I'd say."

"You're dead right Ken, you know we can't create enemies here, it's better to have a fight on our terms and not on another's making."

Keeping close to the trees they rode up the creek and away from confronting the raiders of their camp. Steve looked back to see several men and horses descend upon their abandoned camp.

"Ken I think they've done this before tonight," he voiced a thought.

"Done what?"

"They've intimidated campers into leaving their food on the fires, to leave or else."

"Do you mean we are now part of a stream of people who have been given time to leave, providing the food is left on the fire."

"That's exactly what I mean."

"The ---- bastards."

Steve grinned at Ken's furious voice, "Same here!"

"What can we do about it?"

"Nothing yet, but one day we'll catch them."

Riding out into the moonlight, the creek turned a bend and the raiders were now behind them.

"How far do you want to ride?" Steve asked.

"To a place well away from the scent of cooking meat."

They chose a patch of open country at the end of the long valley and made camp without a fire and ate cold cooked meat. In the morning Ken made a fire to make tea. There was no sign of the raiders.

"Probably still asleep after eating our food," Steve said.

Ken stared into the fire and said, "I want to fight someone."

His companion laughed and agreed, "Me too!"

They both smiled. They were soon back on their horses and riding towards the hills, keeping a sharp lookout for intruders on their path, as they headed in the direction of the high hills.

A day later Steve looked west, saw a settlement and suggested, "It's probably Green Hills, though it looks the opposite to its name."

Ken laughed and told him, "The same can be said of Sergeant Green's settlement of Hill Top, which is situated on flat ground!"

Steve looking north said, "The hills are looking to be densely packed with undergrowth, we'll have to ride between them."

Ken stared downwards and agreed saying, "This is getting to be rough country and we'll become part of the wandering lot of men."

"That might be so, but I'll never give up my freedom again, without a fight," Steve added.

"We both agree on that issue."

They rode down into a valley which was hemmed in on both sides by tall hills, with a creek winding its way between them. They were surprised to see a well-worn track beside the water. In the dust were boot prints, horses hooves and dray wheel prints, all since the last rain, even so they kept an eye out for possible danger.

Ken began to look behind at the hills on either side of the track, a couple of times he stopped riding and sat still listening.

"What's the matter?" Steve asked.

"I don't know, I have that niggling feeling in my back that something isn't right."

"What direction?"

"Behind and in front, I can't tell and it's irritating."

Around the corner of the hill, the track led to a wide-open space between the hills,

"Police," Ken said quietly.

Steve looked behind them and said, "Police coming up behind us too."

"We're trapped Steve and I'm not going to be arrested, if that's what they've got in mind."

"Keep riding Ken until we hear what they want from us."

"It's a ---- set-up"

"Seems like it"

They continued riding at their own pace without a care in the world, towards a man who they soon recognized as a Sergeant. Stopping at a reasonable distance from him, they waited to hear what he had to say. Steve and Ken remained calm as four other police rode up surrounding them.

"Who are you?" The Sergeant asked.

"Out of work stockman," Steve replied

"Where are you heading?"

"North of here."

"Get down off your horses and we'll have a talk," the Sergeant said.

"No, we're quite comfortable where we are now," Ken replied.

One of the police nearest to Ken swung out his arm at him saying, "Get off your bloody horse now!"

Ken grabbed hold of the man's arm and jerked it forward, unseating the unwary policeman who lost his balance and fell to the ground. In an instant the atmosphere changed, Steve rode past the Sergeant and joined Ken on the top side of the police.

"You are both under arrest," the Sergeant said loudly.

"On what charge?" Steve asked .

"Disobeying my order to dismount and riding north.'

"That is a false charge as you well know," Ken said.

"We're leaving," Steve added.

Turning his horse he continued at a steady pace down the valley beside Ken then heard the Sergeant say loudly, "I command you to stop."

Steve and Ken took no notice and continued on their way. Suddenly the unthinkable happened as several shots rang out. The excellent training which both Steve and Ken had received, allowed them to escape injury as their horses fell dead. Both men had hold of their rifles as they fell and now were furiously angry, their horses weren't good ones but they were THEIR horses and didn't deserve to be shot like wild dogs.

Ken aimed his rifle at the approaching police and before firing heard Steve say, "For God's sake shoot to wound but not to kill."

"I'd like to kill that bastard who killed my horse."

"We can't kill them but we can make them suffer."

They did succeed in making the police dive for cover under the trees. Ken and Steve backed into the trees behind them. Looking out at the now vacant track, they suddenly felt something touching their backs and looked around to see two other policemen pointing their guns at them.

"Drop your guns or we fire.'

Neither man obeyed and just stared at the two police.

"Drop them now"

Neither Steve nor Ken moved, nor did they drop their rifles. They didn't hear the approach of the police coming up behind them, nor did they utter a sound when each was hit on the head with something heavy.

Steve regained consciousness to find himself tied up with rope beside Ken also in that state. Ken was bleeding, they'd obviously been badly treated while unconscious. Each had his swag tied to his back. One of the police kicked Ken awake. Steve looked up at the policeman in such a way that sent chills down his spine, not to be intimidated by a prisoner, he kicked Steve for good measure too, after all he was tied up and he had nothing to worry about.

"Get up, you're walking and if you don't walk fast, I'll drag ya," he said.

Steve managed to stop Ken from falling again, he didn't know what they'd done to Ken, but he didn't look well after the second beating. The pull on the long rope kept them at a reasonable pace. They hadn't gone very far, just out of the open space into a narrow one, when a shot rang out and the Sergeant's horse died.

"Halt or a man dies," a voice called out.

The police looked around at the thick undergrowth fearfully.

There was another shout, "Drop your weapons now."

There was a clatter of rifles hitting the ground and masked men rode out of the trees. Steve counted at least eight men heavily armed and well fed. The leader rode down the line of police until he came to the one holding the rope. Without any warning he punched the man in the jaw so hard he lost his balance and fell from his saddle, jerking the rope as he was falling, as he let go of it. Both Steve and Ken fell into the dust. The leader made a sign to one of his men, who dismounted and went to where Steve and Ken were sitting and cut the rope. Ken had to be helped by Steve to stand up, no one spoke a word, as the man helped them up onto a police horse. The silence sent chills down their spines, there was death in the cold faces. The Sergeant managed to get clear of his horse as it fell, but not without getting hurt, now he was limping and being helped by one of his policemen.

The leader looked down at the Sergeant and said, "You won't be needing these two prisoners anymore. Out of work stockmen treated like dangerous men, what's the world coming to?"

The Sergeant with spirit told him what he thought the world was coming to with criminals interfering with the police. The leader laughed as he and his men rode away with Steve and Ken with them. In moments they had vanished into thick undergrowth.

Chapter 11

Sergeant Ray Shaw, who was in charge of the Green Hills barracks, watched as the masked men rode into the thick scrub and vanished from sight. Two of his men noticed that he didn't look disturbed at their disappearance. Perhaps he was still shocked at the willful shooting of his horse. The Sergeant turned and called out to Mr. Swan and Mr. Willow who duly walked across to where he was standing.

"Please gather up all the saddles and equipment from the dead horses and load them on to two horses," he instructed them.

"Does that mean three men will be walking back to the barracks?" Andrew Willow asked.

"Yes Mr. Willow, that's the correct assessment of the situation in which we find ourselves, and I'm riding a horse."

It didn't take long to pack the two horses and begin the trip back to the barracks. Ted Swan smiled as he listened to the grumblings from the four police who had been sent from the other side of the Blue Mountains, to assist in this operation. Neither Andrew nor Ted understood why other police had been engaged for this job, when the Green Hills police could've done it just as well.

"Why did you fire at the horses?" the Sergeant asked Andrew.

"Ted and I aimed for the men and both the horses heads rose up at the same time, we think it was a snake which caused them to shy. It was an accident and made those criminals furious."

"Do you blame them?"

"No, and we had to deal with them harshly."

"So it wasn't intentional on your part?"

"We were both shocked at the death of the horses, it's a pity we didn't get the men instead," Ted answered.

"Do you think that's why the leader of those crooks shot your horse, because he'd thought you had ordered the killing of those two horses?" Andrew enquired.

"Yes, I believe you're correct."

It was widely known that the Sergeant loved his horse and wouldn't let anyone else ride her. He remained quiet for the rest of the ride back to Green Hills.

Andrew listened as the other men talked about having to walk, they couldn't understand about the concern of shooting the horses.

"By the looks of the horses those criminals were riding, they should've gone to the knacker's yard a long time ago," one of the men commented.

Ted lent down towards him and said, "Men love their horses and you say those words softly, unless you want a sore jaw."

To which the policeman replied, "F--- hell, I'll be glad to get home."

The Sergeant had heard those words and felt anger rising. He could hardly wait to get rid of the four police. In time they would be informed about this operation, but not until it was over. He felt a certain degree of pleasure that three of these had to walk the several miles as the 'crow flies', back to the barracks. Once back on his home turf, he thanked the visiting police and suggested they get a good night's sleep for an early start in the morning to return home.

Sergeant Shaw had a verbal report to make to the Special Operational Team. Even though he was in his own district, Sergeant Green was also involved, having sent a number of his police to assist in gathering information. Now was the time to inform Mr. Swan and Mr. Willow about the operation.

"There will be a meeting in my office this evening that I require you to be present at. What you will hear is strictly confidential. Do you understand?" he said when they were alone at the stables.

"Yes Sergeant"

He was feeling irritated because he couldn't walk without a stick and Ted found one for him and received a short reply as he hobbled to his office, leaving his two police wondering 'what was in the wind'. Ted and Andrew had wondered why there were police operating in their district who didn't attend the office.

They presented themselves at the office at the required time, to see a couple of men in civilian clothes, along with other police they'd met some weeks ago: Ian Percy, Bill Todd and John Hale.

"These men are from the city on a Special Assignment, Mr. Alex Pitt and Mr. Charley Rush," their Sergeant said introducing the men two men out of uniform.

"What have you to report?" he asked, turning to Alex.

"Charley and I have been talking in camps about the two men who are out of work stockmen, riding in this direction as bad men. Obviously word has reached the desired place, because we watched the men rescue them from you today."

"Mr. Rush have you anything to add to Mr. Pitt's report"

"No, we lost them in the thick undergrowth. I don't know what was done to the two men, but I think Ken was unconscious, which isn't good for the outcome we want for this job."

"Anything else?"

"We picked up a story that a man has been killed for attempting to escape in a particularly nasty way, and everyone had to watch his death," Charley said quietly.

"How did he die?" the sergeant asked.

"Meat ants."

The room of men became silent and John said softly, "And we've sent two of our colleagues into that hellhole."

"Where is Tony Bane?" the Sergeant asked.

"He was shadowing Steve and Ken but they gave him the slip!"

"How did it go today, from what we saw it didn't look good at the end," Alex asked the Sergeant.

"How are Steve and Ken?" Ian asked.

"Why would you know the names of two out of work stockmen?" Ted asked, before anyone could answer.

"They're not out of work stockmen," Alex explained.

"Who are they?" Andrew whispered in a dawning knowledge

"They're undercover policemen," Alex continued.

Andrew and Ted looked shocked.

"Sergeant I think we ought to have been told at least part of this story. You are well aware that Ted and I are good at keeping secrets. There will be bad blood between those two men and us," Andrew stated.

"Explain please Andrew?" Alex asked.

"We thought they were criminals and during the arrest shot their horses."

There was a shocked silence in the office, before Alex continued, "Explain."

They did so to a silent group of men who now talked about a snake being in the wrong place at the wrong time, which could upset an operation.

"If you'd seen their faces you would've known they were dangerous men, it was them or us," Ted added.

"What happened next?"

Andrew glanced at his Sergeant who said, "Carry on, you didn't know, so you can't be held responsible."

"They were knocked out from behind, they would've died before they would've surrendered. While they were unconscious, the other police gave them a rough time. We watched as they laid their boots into them. One man was tough and the other not so, but who cared, they were criminals."

"Did you take Steve's knives from him?" Ian asked quietly.

"What knives?"

"If they'd really been crooks you'd be dead now. Steve is a master at throwing knives and he keeps two of them secreted amongst his clothes," Ian grinned and explained.

Andrew changed colour and looking at his Sergeant said, "You should have warned us."

"This is news to me, why wasn't I told Mr. Percy?"

"They needed to have some advantage over the arresting police!"

"I don't find this funny at all."

"Sergeant Shaw, they were undercover police, when they fired their rifles at you they knew they couldn't kill you but could put a bullet into an arm or leg."

"I don't find your words reassuring, as several of those men will need some medical attention after today's field work. I'll have to explain to their senior officer why they are in this condition."

"Whereas they have put our special operation into serious jeopardy," Alex added.

"Why couldn't we have been told who they were, if we'd known we wouldn't have allowed them to be beaten up," Andrew replied.

"Our problem was and is to keep the operation as secret as possible, the more people who know, the higher the possibility of the opposition finding out. Andrew you know that as well as we do," Bill answered.

"What happens now?" Ted asked.

"We wait to hear what transpires in the future," Alex replied.

"There is one thing that has come out of this unholy mess, they will never believe those two men are undercover police the way they were beaten up, it just might work out in our favour," Charley added cheerfully.

Chapter 12

The men stopped riding about half an hour after rescuing Steve and Ken from the police. The leader of the band of men approached the two horses where they were being held by two of his men. Ken was barely conscious and had to be held in a firm grasp and Steve was concerned for his welfare.

"We have to blindfold you, it is a sack and extends to the waist, don't worry about it, it is only for a short time," the leader said.

They endured the suffocating blindfold for a considerable time, Steve felt a deep penetrating cold as if he was underground and was wise enough to keep silent. Ken wouldn't have known where he was other than on a horse, and knew he had to remain quiet, as their lives depended upon it. Steve was concerned that the cold could make Ken's health worse than it already was at the present time, so when at last he felt the warm rays of the sun it was with relief. A little while later the waist length blindfolds were removed and he saw he was in a valley with steep stone cliffs on either side of it, with thick growth at each end of the valley and along the top of the cliffs, creating an enclosed place, hidden from the world outside. Steve now understood why it couldn't be located by the police.

This assessment was done in seconds and hadn't been noticed by any of the men. To those who had rescued them, Steve only showed an interest in Ken's welfare. He was distinctly aware of being under observation and he knew those who watched would later interpret to others how he had behaved. This was enemy territory. It wasn't just a wall of cliffs, it was also a wall of men, desperate to maintain their existence in this enclosed community, or at least those in control of the valley kept an iron control of it.

The leader took them down the valley to a slab hut and pulled up his horse outside it, and called out, "Come out you old bastard, I've got two fellows to share your roof, don't keep me waiting for ever."

An old man with grey hair came to the door of the hut and lent against it, saying, "What do you want with me Richards?"

"I've got two new men to live with you."

"I thought there was room up at the barracks."

"One of them is sick, beaten up by the police, better to be here than with us."

"Richards," the man said, "I live on my own and I'll not be bothered by any of the garbage you bring into the valley."

The man Richards looked furious at being spoken to like this in front of his men and a nasty expression passed over his face.

"One day Kevin you'll have an accident, and you'll take a long time to die," he said with a laugh.

"The man won't be happy."

"He'll believe me, as he always does now, your day is over old man."

While they were talking Steve alighted from the horse, the man in the saddle made no effort to help, nor had he spoken one word since Steve had climbed up on to the back of the horse after the rescue. Equally they'd made no effort to assist Ken either on or off his horse, Steve had helped him both times. Now, standing to one side, Ken barely conscious leaning heavily against Steve, waited silently for Richards and Kevin to finish their confrontation. This ended quite suddenly after Kevin had said, "One day the man will learn the truth and you will feed the meat ants."

"And f--- you old man."

Jerking his bridle, he turned his horse and rode back down the valley, followed by his men. Kevin watched them leave with a smile and turned to Steve.

"Bring your mate inside, there's some old bags he can use for the time being. What's his name?" he said.

"Ken, and I'm Steve."

"What can you do?"

"We're out of work stockmen so we can do most things as required.'

"What kind of a welcome did Richards give you."

"He told me that if Ken doesn't make it there is a graveyard here and if I f--- up I can join him," Steve smiled and replied.

"Cheerful sort he is, Steve. He's a right bastard and make no mistake about it, keep out of his way if you can avoid him."

"We don't want any problems Kevin if we can avoid creating a fight."

"I thought by the look of you, you'd do well in the ring or in a street fight."

"I've done a bit of fighting, but I don't look for it."

"Well, you don't want to fight here, because it's dirty, anything goes, no rules and no fair play.'

Steve grinned at Kevin and expressed cheerfully, "I can fight that game any way it comes!"

"You'll have choices Steve, and I hope you make the right ones." Kevin mused.

"I come from a man's world and I rarely back away from injustice when it is close to me."

"Can you milk a cow?" Kevin asked.

"As many as you like!" He laughed and replied.

"I'm responsible for the cows and milking. You are new men and if you are wise you can talk to me as much as you like, but no one else. Death by the meat-ants is nasty to watch," Kevin said.

"Do we have to watch it?" Steve asked.

"Yes, anyone who refuses is likely to be the next candidate, Richards is a cruel bastard. Never ever give him an opportunity or he will take Ken and make you watch."

"Does he have a following here?"

"Yes, as long as he's alive!"

Kevin shared his food and watched as Steve lifted Ken up on his arm and fed him carefully, tipping a mug of lukewarm tea into his mouth. Kevin noted that for an obviously hard man, Steve was also gentle with his sick mate. It was a plus in his eyes as he noted Steve's behaviour in and around the hut.

The next morning Steve had to leave Ken in Kevin's care, when one of the men who also did the milking came to get him. Kevin introduced him as Jackson and as they walked away from the hut Jackson asked, "Are you the new man who got rescued?"

"Yes, and my mate who was badly beaten up by those bastards."

"It happens sometimes. We do the milking early in the morning."

Jackson was a slim man and mostly silent and gave the impression of strength if required, not a man to mess around without care. Kevin was also a slim man and strong, but he had kind eyes whereas Jackson had eyes as cold as a frosty morning. Jackson obviously liked the cows and treated them with kindness, perhaps a memory from childhood in another life. Steve was pleased he had been taught to milk cows at Red's place, as this was his first job, and he was being watched by several men. These men had arrived with empty buckets, his job was to fill them with milk. He refrained from asking any questions, though he was curious.

"Very wise not to ask where the milk is going, this isn't a good place to be curious, not if you want to live in comfort." Jackson said as he saw his expression of curiosity.

"I'm happy to do my work and keep an eye on my friend Ken," Steve replied.

"I hear he isn't doing so well."

"He'll be better in a day or two."

"Keep him away from the alcohol, more than one mug is lethal."

"Thanks for telling me, he doesn't drink much alcohol but loves a mug of tea."

One job followed another and he won a shout of laughter from some men when an old goat charged him and he didn't get out of the road quickly enough! Steve made himself relax and take whatever came his way during the day. At night when he returned to the hut, Kevin confirmed his thoughts, as he looked down at his friend lying still near the open doorway.

"Your friend is barely conscious, and I reckon his cold will soon break, I'm here to keep him company."

There was not much Steve could do other than be as useful as he was able in helping Kevin. The next day Kevin sat beside the sick man and was getting him to drink some ale, when in his delirium Ken began to talk clearly for a few moments, before descending into a ramble of words again. Kevin was deeply shocked and disturbed at what he had heard but decided to keep the knowledge that they were undercover police officers to himself. Nor would he let on that he knew their secret. Kevin decided to watch and see what sort of men they would turn out to be?

The flu broke and his breathing became normal and within a couple of days Ken was able to sit in the sun and eat a better meal. A day or so later Ken was able to join Steve in the milking shed. Kevin gave no indication that he was watching the two men, but he didn't miss much in his hut. He soon recognized that he enjoyed them and relaxed in their company.

Kevin admired courage and as he came to know Steve and Ken in the weeks since they had arrived, he thought they were enormously courageous to enter a valley with an evil reputation not knowing that it was almost impossible to leave of their own volition. He thought they were unique men and wondered what was in store for them in this valley.

"You will be working with Dommy today when you've finished milking. His real name is Dominic, but we all call him Dommy because he is easy to get on, not like some men." Kevin called to Steve.

"What will I be doing today?"

"Dommy will be cutting up several kangaroos for our supply of meat."

"Is there a problem involved?"

"Yes, Richards takes the best cuts. Don't argue, hand them over."

"Must I?"

"Yes, you'll have to fight him one day, but not over the meat."

Dommy was a cheerful man in his early thirties, short and overweight as expected of the cook. The killing was done quickly and the animals soon skinned. Richards came and demanded his favourite cuts as usual, and Steve gave them to him in silence.

"I've been hearing bits about you and I don't like it, I'm going to cut you down to size one day and feed you to my f—dog," Richards said glaring at Steve.

"In your dreams Richards"

There was a nasty look, and he turned away carrying his meat. It wasn't in Steve's nature to turn away from a bully and Richards kept niggling at him at every opportunity. Soon the men began to notice that every time Steve and Richards met invisible sparks flew between them, and it caused talk.

Kevin pulled Steve aside one morning and voiced his concern, "Steve, you are going to have to fight him, and it will be to the death. Make sure you win."

"Is there any way out of it?"

"You know there isn't any other solution."

"What will happen if he kills me?"

"Ken will go to the ants for sure."

"But why Kevin?"

"He can't afford to leave an enemy in the camp."

"I see, I do understand the complications if I fail to kill him."

Kevin continued to explain, "You'll not only be fighting Richards, but all his friends at the same time. This is how he fights, so you will need to slice any man who gets close to you."

"I don't want his position; I'm quite happy milking cows and doing odd jobs."

"That isn't the way this valley operates Steve. You have to play by our expectations or

you will not survive the Summer."

This conversation gave Steve and Ken a lot to talk about in private, they both liked Kevin, and Steve decided to only fight Richards if Kevin was threatened in any way. The days passed and turned into weeks and gradually they wondered who consumed all the milk produced each day.

When Ken began to speak about it Kevin stopped him, "Ken, not a word. This is a no- go subject, never ask. Just milk the cows and watch the buckets leave. Not one word to those taking the buckets.'

"You're very serious about it Kevin."

"It's death you're playing with here, every day and at night in the hut, it is another day I've survived, get real Ken."

While they were talking three weeks later after doing the milking, Richards came along riding his horse, neither man moved to open the gate to let him through it. Richards demanded a mug of fresh milk, there was none available and Kevin told him it had all gone in buckets. Ken reluctantly opened the gate, and he rode through to a patch of open ground.

Kevin had turned his back and was walking to his hut, when suddenly Richards said furiously, "I'll teach you to turn your f--- back on me you old bastard."

In the next moment his whip sailed out to Kevin's back, it was so unexpected that Kevin let out a cry of pain, as he turned to face his assailant and shouted, "You f—bastard."

As quick as a flash Steve ran forward and grabbed the whip and yanked it hard, unseating Richards who fell awkwardly from his horse. He scrambled to his feet, furious and having difficulty getting the words out of his mouth with Steve standing near him holding the end of the whip.

Richards, who was still tugging his whip handle, spluttered, "I'll make you pay for that you f—bastard"

Steve didn't let go of the whip and pulled hard on it, causing Richards to stumble forward as Steve roared at him.

"How dare you whip Kevin for not being able to give you any milk, when you know quite well it's all gone elsewhere."

Richards was almost beside himself in uncontrolled anger and lashed out with his tongue.

"You think you're good don't you. I'll teach you, while taking the skin off you're back."

"Richards, you couldn't fight your way out of a tent, let alone face a man, you can always try, I'd say you've got the blood of a coward in your veins."

"You've done it now Steve," Kevin said.

"I hope so Kevin."

Richards, almost beyond reason, spluttered out, "I'll fight you now you f---bastard and I'll watch you die slowly."

His friends tried to stop the proposed fight, but he wouldn't listen, mumbling to himself about killing Steve.

"FIGHT BOYS," Kevin shouted out loudly.

Men seemed to rise out of the tall grass as Ken wondered where they'd all come from to watch the fight. He also noticed a change come over Steve, as the civilized veneer of what he had become as a policeman, vanished to be replaced by a street fighter. Ken watched fascinated at the change and began to feel a lot happier in Steve's ability to win. Kevin had also noticed the change and like Ken, felt that at last Richards had met his match in this man from another world.

Richards had begun to circle Steve with slightly bent knees, knife in one hand, the other out for balance. Steve watched the eyes of his enemy, hardly daring to blink, like the eyes of a snake. The tension grew and Steve was aware of several men with knives in their hands. Steve thought to himself so that's how men fight here and how other men have lost their lives in fighting Richards. He smiled with real amusement and the men who held knives in their hands felt a cold shiver down their spines. They instinctively recognised a different type of man. A couple of the men stepped back into the crowd, out of range of his knife. Richards saw them move and called out, "You F--- bastards, how dare you leave me, cut him or I'll cut you later."

Turning to Steve he continued, "I'll cut your balls and feed them to my dogs while you watch."

"I'll be surprised if you have any balls, Richards. If I can locate any, the crows can have them," Steve laughed cheerfully,

The crowd of men laughed, and Richards scowled at them, muttering under his breath at what was in store for them later. He was now red in the face and lashed out with his knife, startled not to find flesh, whereas Steve sliced his balance arm. One of the men behind Steve raised his arm with a knife. Steve saw Richards eyes raised and knew what was about to happen and, in an instant, he moved like lightning and sliced the man's arm, who let out a yell. The others, who may have had similar ideas, backed into the crowd, well away from the knife.

Richards' second in command in the lower valley, known as Joe, backed away from the circle of fighting men. Richards saw and called out, "I always knew you were a F—coward Joe, you're a dead man when I've finished with this piece of shit."

"I reckon there's going to be a change of command around here in a minute or two," one man called out.

The men moved well back from their old leader, as he screamed abuse at them, all the time bleeding from new wounds, which were being constantly inflicted by Steve's relentless attacks. It was a fair fight on the whole, no one was able to interfere in anyway. The end came suddenly with a straight lunge through an unguarded space to the heart. Steve drew back holding his knife dripping with blood, as Richard's knife fell from his dying hand and his eyes glazed over as he fell to the bloody grass.

A sigh rose from the men as Joe stepped forward to face Steve saying, "Do you accept me as the new leader?"

"Yes Joe."

"Good, because I don't want to have to kill you, one step out of line and you're a dead man. Do you understand me?"

"Yes Joe."

"Good."

He turned to a couple of men and ordered, "Take this bag of shit, strip him and give him to the ants. It will save you from digging a hole."

They hurried to comply with his commands, while Joe turned again to face Steve with a hard stare into his eyes. No word was spoken, and Steve understood the silence. They were opponents, simply because he had beaten Richards in a fair fight. Just like on the streets where Steve had learnt to fight and now it was happening all over again.

Steve made the gesture by saying, "I know what you're thinking Joe."

"I thought you might know."

"I don't want your job; I'm quite happy living with Kevin and Ken."

"As long as we understand each other, there are no second chances with me.'

"Nor me Joe."

"Keep out of my way and we'll get on fine."

"Agreed."

Joe didn't like Steve having the last word as he picked up Richards discarded whip and mounted his own horse. One of his men handed him the reins of Richards horse, now his property, and rode away. Steve could have claimed the horse, but wisely let Joe take it. This act was noted by Joe, who would owe something to Steve in the future, which intensely irritated him, as he didn't want to owe him anything. Steve knew what Joe would be thinking, as he'd been in the same position at one time and smiled as he walked to Kevin's hut.

Kevin met him outside under the tree where there were a few stumps around a larger one making a table. Ken was already seated with mugs of tea on the table.

"I'm glad you put Richards out of the way, he was a nasty piece of work." Kevin said.

"Joe's not much different; power creates the desire for more power and all the nasties that go with it."

Ken expressed his thoughts, "I don't understand Steve."

"You grew up on a farm Ken. I grew up on a street. In killing Richards, I have proved myself capable of holding my own in this valley. This in turn is a challenge to Joe. He won't be fully in charge until I'm dead. This is a straight assessment of the situation, is it not Kevin?'

"Quite correct Steve and you'll have to watch yourself every day from now onwards. Make no mistake Ken, we'll have to be wary of strangers who will be seeking to be friends with Joe."

Ken was now deeply disturbed at the possibility of something happening to his friend, Steve wasn't just his colleague. They needed to get the information required and leave before another fight.

"It was a good fight Steve," Kevin spoke with respect.

"I enjoyed it, Kevin."

Steve sipped the hot tea and asked him, "How long do you think I've got before he'll want to settle this matter."

There was silence as the old man gazed into the fire and reluctantly spoke quietly, "I reckon probably late Summer or when Joe feels he can beat you in a fight, proving he is the better man."

"I think Joe will be a dirty fighter as Richards was in his fight, This time Joe will have support from the men who will want him to win," Steve mused.

"You're right about having men who will be supporting him, you won't be able to win."

Ken who had been listening to this interchange asked Kevin, "What chance does Steve have in surviving such a fight?"

He looked up from gazing into the fire and spoke with regret, "No chance Ken."

There was silence as Kevin stirred the hot coals sending a shower of sparks into the air.

"Ken, late Summer is months away, so we won't worry about something which might never happen. Joe might get bitten by a snake!" Steve spoke quietly.

They laughed and Ken replied, "The snake's bite probably wouldn't kill him because it is one snake to another one!"

Steve turned to face Kevin and asked. "What did Richards do which the man won't like when he hears about it?"

"You don't miss much do you Steve?"

"What did he do?"

"As I told you, when we first came here, we had the run of the entire valley, and it was a grand hide-out. The man came and with his men took control of our lives, those who opposed him were permanently removed, It happened suddenly and as you have found out, none of us are allowed to go near either ends of the valley. Richards did go and he raped one of the women who work on the northern end.'

"Didn't she report it?" Steve asked.

"Who to, not in this place. He hurt her quite badly I was told, it interfered with her work and the man wouldn't have liked it."

"The man wouldn't have liked her being raped or it interfering with her work?" Ken enquired thoughtfully.

"Work of course, she as a person doesn't come into it at all," Kevin looked at Ken and answered.

"What is her work?" Steve asked curiously.

A change came over Kevin, all humour vanished from his face, and he replied in a toneless voice, "I've heard rumours which I don't want to believe, so let's say I don't know anything," then added, "One day it might change, but not yet. Now it's time to get back to work."

Ken followed Steve to the milking shed to clean it up for the next day. One job followed another with various conversations with different men they met each day. Some were happy to talk, and others avoided all communication. One way and another they met men who worked in the lower valley, hearing many whispers about the secret work. But not one whisper about where the women worked.

"A long time ago a man did investigate and was caught, we were forced to watch his brutal murder, I was only young at the time. We keep quiet now and keep as far away from that place as possible. To ask is to die," Dommy told Ken.

"What about the other place?"

"We know what is happening there and we don't talk about it either," Dommy grinned.

"But why Dommy?"

"It hurts if we get caught."

"I've seen men with stumps instead of hands."

Dommy paled and nodded.

"Not a word will pass my lips, I promise," Ken said.

Dommy smiled and changed the subject. Ken liked him and never again asked dangerous questions. He was a happy companion on the jobs which Ken assisted him, also a fountain of information. He loved to gossip about what he heard as the cook of the main community of the men at the central huts. In this way Ken learnt a good deal about the lawless men of the valley. Fights were frequent in the huts, they left Dommy alone because he was such a good cook. Regardless of their other vices, they loved their food. There was no doubt about the cruel streak in the men. Dommy repeated what he had recently heard while handing out plates of food to Ken, while they were cutting up meat.

"There is speculation about who will be the next victim to visit the ants and stay with them. I don't like that kind of talk, it's unsettling."

Ken agreed with him.

Some weeks passed in relative peace, until the cows broke through a fence and wandered over the valley floor to a green patch of grass near a clump of trees. Steve was sent to bring them back and, in the process, saw dray wheel tracks leading into a seemingly wall of growth. He wanted to investigate, when he heard his name shouted with the words, "Come here now."

It was Joe demanding his presence. He walked across the open ground to where he was standing

"What are you doing up here?"

"Rounding up the cows"

"How did they get out?"

"They broke through the fence and Kevin sent me to bring them back again."

Steve had been avoiding Joe since the fight and was careful not to give him any reason to attack either himself or Ken, so he was respectful to Joe.

"What were you looking at on the ground over there?"

"Hoof marks, to see if I had to go into the bush to find them."

"Did you find any marks?"

"Not sure, there's a fair bit of grass near those trees."

Joe wasn't happy, he wanted to have a reason to start a fight, but not today, and said, "You herd up the cows and I'll go and have a look in the bush."

Steve returned and gradually drew the cows into a herd, while Joe flushed out an old one from the bush. Joe had to stamp his authority and said bluntly, "This area is out of bounds to you, get those F—cows back down where they belong, and if I see you up here again, I'll take a whip to you."

Steve bowed his head in submission to Joe and walked back following the cows to the hole in the fence. Kevin and Ken were fixing it as the cows passed through the broken area. The next time the cows broke through the fence, it was Joe's friends who were responsible. A couple of them tried to jump over the fence and the horses didn't cooperate and went through it, scattering the cows south, which was also out of bounds to Steve. Joe was angry and he blasted everyone but his friends. He sent Steve down to retrieve them saying, "Get those F--- cows up here now."

Steve hastened to obey and was able to get a good view of the operation through the trees, it was a quick glance to get a good idea of the set-up. The cows obligingly wandered where he was forbidden to go in normal circumstances. Steve made full use of this opportunity and noted many secrets. Slowly the cows answered his voice and wandered back having enjoyed their freedom yet again.

Both Steve and Ken were aware of the passing of time as the Summer was coming to an end, as yet they had found no way out of the valley. It was a fortress, and they talked quietly amongst themselves about this problem.

"What are we going to do Steve?" Ken asked.

"I believe something will turn up; it always does you know."

"I've never liked the waiting!"

"Ken, we have no choice but to wait and both see and hear what our options are to be." "You're very calm about it."

"Don't worry, we have made friends here, I'm sure we will get help if we need it."

Chapter 13

Several weeks after Steve and Ken had been taken into the valley, Ian Percy and Bill Todd were called to a meeting, which was held at a campsite away from prying eyes. Bill and Ian had a fire burning for tea when the man who called the meeting arrived. He was a government agent, who said his name was Abel. He'd obviously been undercover on a poor-quality horse, shabbily attired and Ian thought he'd not bathed for a week as he also had an unfortunate body odour. Ian automatically stood up wind from where Abel was standing.

"You needn't be so squeamish about me." Abel said, noticing Ian's movement.

"You're an example of the great unwashed."

"And F—you too."

"Not at this hour of the morning!"

"Cut it out you two," Bill chipped in, adding to Abel, "Have you found the trail yet?"

"No unfortunately, but recently a large number of counterfeit coins have been circulating in the coastal areas. This is the fourth batch we've located in the last two years. These are of better quality than the earlier ones.'

"Any definite change?" Ian asked.

"Yes, gold sovereigns."

"What are they like?"

"The same as the other coins, same weight, except the gold wears off in a short period of time."

"Do the general public know about it, I haven't heard a whisper about it," Bill enquired.

"No, we thought we could locate the problem and stop it before it got out of hand."

"Have there been many gold sovereigns made?" Ian asked.

"No, but they are improving, with more added gold."

"Real gold?" Bill asked.

"Yes, he must have a source of it."

"What do you want us to do Abel?" Ian asked.

"We know these coins are being made somewhere in the north, we think it could be in the valley where you have an investigation operating. We also think the man who seems to own the valley is responsible for the counterfeit ones."

"I'd put several coins on you!" Bill intervened saying.

"Very likely they'd be counterfeit ones!" Ian laughed.

"That would be okay if I was paying you!" Bill replied.

Abel didn't have a sense of humour and said briskly, "This isn't a joking matter. We need you to check the contents of all the drays being driven from the coast, noting their destination. We are particularly interested in drays which have heavy loads, with the rims of the drays sinking into the ground."

"I wouldn't have thought many people would have a use for the gold coins." Bill thought out loud.

"You'd be surprised the number of these coins that are circulating in the community." Abel explained.

"Not out here." Bill said.

"Of course out here, everywhere, not every person is like the police using the small coins like a truepenny-bit or shillings," Abel said with a sigh of irritation.

Abel finished his tea and without another word left the campsite, much to the relief of the policemen.

"This is a job for Tony Bane and John Hale. I think we need to have a chat to the Hunt Brothers too, they always know about the other Carriers," Ian suggested.

"Who else are we meeting away from Green Hills?"

"Sergeant Shaw informed me that we are to meet a couple of city police, who are also undercover. He seemed to think we might be able to help them on another matter, but he didn't explain what they wanted from us.'

"We have Sergeant Ray Shaw here at Green Hills, and the other Sergeant Shaw whom we saw killed. Funny old world isn't it?' Bill's mind wandered away as he mused.

"Yes it is. I heard that crooked Shaw was a cousin of his on another branch of his extensive family."

Ian stood up and began to put out the fire with water.

"We're not going to find those drays if we stay here chatting. We'd better go and hear what these city police want from us," he said.

"Where are they now?"

"Alex was the source of Sergeant's request, they contacted him by chance in a camp east of here out of uniform."

"Yes, but where are we going?"

"About a day's ride east on the main track leading to the Blue Mountains. You know the camp where you once said it would be nice spot to build a house," Ian replied.

"So that's the place where this meeting is to take place."

It was a comfortable ride along the track with men, women and hordes of children walking from one gold mining site to another. Some overburdened carts had broken down, and always there were people milling about offering a hand or helping themselves to other people's goods. Having a police presence kept the thieves at bay for a short time, and curses when they were out of sight.

The area where Bill thought it would be nice to live was on a rise, above a creek with a clear view of the distant mountains. It was away from the main road and the constant cloud of dust rising from the feet of the many tramping on it. As they approached they saw two men come out from behind the tall trees, to a small campfire surrounded by stones which had been gathered by Bill the last time he'd been here.

The men had obviously been here for several days using it as a base camp, never leaving anything behind each day as was the custom in the bush then returning at night. Bill rode up to the camp, alighted and introduced Ian and himself.

A tall man stepped forward saying, "Paddy Morris and my colleague Gavin Hawke, the billy has boiled," which was always a good indication of friendliness.

There was small talk as each man summed up the other, until the first mugs of tea had vanished.

"Alex Pitt asked us to come and talk to you about a problem," Ian said.

Paddy looked at Gavin and asked, "Do you want to answer him?"

"Yes. Alex, Paddy and I joined at the same time. We've worked on and off with each other for years. He suggested we have a chat to you."

Paddy grinned at Gavin and said, "Get on with it!"

"As you heard, my friend likes to get to the point without an introduction. We're trying to find missing street children, we've been up and down the coastline for the last few years. No sign of them anywhere," Gavin continued.

"What street children?" Bill asked.

"These are the urchins who have been turned out to fend for themselves, what they can steal they sell and if desperate, they sell themselves," Paddy answered.

Gavin took up the story, "Mostly they are a nuisance to all the stall holders in the

streets. They steal to live. When they vanish it's a big relief, except for the few kind people who give them food and shelter in old stables or warehouses."

"A couple of years ago one of these kind men reported an entire group of children had

vanished without a trace. He went searching and found no sign of them," Paddy added.

"What did the police do?" Bill asked.

"Nothing at the time, relieved that the little thieves had gone. Then there were more reports of missing children over the next two years. After that we were ordered to investigate."

"I don't understand why Alex put you on to us?" Bill enquired again.

"Paddy you tell him," Gavin replied.

"But it's only a legend, it can't be true. You tell him."

"Oh! All right. There is a story about two street urchins who had been turned out into the street to fend for themselves. They were given shelter by a working prostitute, who used her spare shillings to send them to school. These two boys were taught to speak English in a better way than on the street. Later they joined the Police, I tell you it's only a story, told in the grog shops, it couldn't happen in real life."

Both Paddy and Gavin fell silent as the saw the grins on Ian and Bill's faces.

"So that's their background, we knew some of it," Bill said to Ian.

"Is it a true story?" Gavin asked in surprise.

"Yes it's a true story," Bill replied'

"Where are they now?" Paddy asked.

"They're with us, they came from the city, so you can't have asked the right police about the story."

"If that was their background they would've kept it a secret and not told anyone, not even the recruiting Sergeant," Gavin speculated.

Paddy was still amazed and commented, "I wonder what they know about the missing children?"

"Are they bright young men?" Gavin asked.

"Yes and good at learning fast, soaking up knowledge like the best of us," Bill laughed and said.

"Can we talk to them please?" Paddy asked.

"No, not for some time, they're both engaged in a Special operation of a secret nature, of which we can't talk about," Ian replied carefully.

"We won't ask what they're doing. Some of our colleagues are also doing secret work, like what Charley Rush and Alex Pitt are doing at the present time," Gavin said quietly, looking into the fire.

Ian re-affirmed his and Bill's position by saying, "We can't talk about it. I suggest you meet up again with Alex and Charley."

"I'll say one thing, you bush police shup up like clams and don't help your city colleagues," Paddy grinned in an effort to take the sting out of his next words, then added, "After all they are just f--- street kids playing at being police."

"Paddy that's unfair and you know it, they have the right to better themselves," Gavin snapped.

"Not in my book, a F—street kid sitting beside me! No, I'd arrest them for acting as policemen."

This was too much for Bill, who said, "Paddy if you so much as attempted to do that, we would lock you up and throw away the key. Whether you like it or not they are fully qualified policemen."

"I'd be careful Paddy, one if not both of them are courting a squatter's twin daughters. You won't be fit to sit beside either of them in time, it will be the kitchen fire for you," Ian added.

"I bet they haven't told them people about their adopted Mother being an old pro."

"You're wrong about that too. You're as bad as Charley, he has one half of a woodheap on his shoulder and you have the other half!!" Ian replied.

"For god's sake shut-up, it's that F--- foreign blood in you that makes you so unreasonable and disagreeable at times," Gavin said to Paddy.

"You leave my ancestors out of it, my parents were properly married, not like the street kids."

"There is no proof Paddy that the parents were not married." Bill commented.

Gavin was tempted to enter into this fruitless conversation but refrained, as it would be a long ride back to the city if Paddy was in a bad mood, and by every indication he would be a difficult companion.

"Do I assume the two men in question will not be returning to the city, when the Special Operation is completed," he asked Ian.

"That's correct."

"Are you able to help at all?"

"Yes, this matter will be referred to Alex and Charley. They'll contact you if we discover any missing children."

Gavin mounted his horse and wished Bill and Ian a cheerful farewell, which was returned in equal measure. Paddy raised an arm and rode away towards the Blue Mountains, followed by Gavin.

"What made you decide to encourage them to leave now for the city, with only a few hours of daylight left in the day?" Bill asked.

"We need time to think about this knew information concerning our two friends."

"What have you in mind?" Bill enquired.

"A question came into my mind as they were talking about the men, which hasn't risen until now."

"Do you mean how they became involved in this operation in the first place, and our police were gradually moved aside?"

"Yes, exactly. I believe Gavin knows more about them than we do. It's a sore point with Paddy."

"We'll probably never find out, their past will be well and truly buried now. If their work succeeds it's a feather in our caps, if it fails there will be bodies to bury and the matter will be closed. Did they really tell the Gill's about their Mother being on the game?"

"I don't know. Paddy irritated me!" Ian grinned.

"We'll have a talk to Alex about it the next time we meet to report information," Bill laughed.

Chapter 14

Meanwhile Tony Bane and John Hale were riding along the road, which was little more than a track, leading down a hill, with thick growth either side of it. Turning a corner they came upon a cart which had turned over, spreading the owners possessions all over the road. The older woman was deeply distressed as she and her younger girls tried to put everything back into the cart, now standing upright beside the road.

She looked around counting her children and said loudly, "One is missing, where's Dicky?"

"He went down there," an older girl said, pointing in the direction that her young brother had gone.

John, who had arrived in time to hear these words, asked her, "Do you want me to go down and find him for you?"

Tony, who had been with John long enough to know his kind nature, smiled and said, "Go on John, down you go!"

He alighted from his horse and handed the reins to Tony, then walked down into the thick undergrowth, wondering where that unwashed kid had got to. Suddenly he broke through a thick curtain of growth, to find himself standing on a well-used track with the little boy standing in the middle of it. John, after greeting the boy, walked to the other side and looking down saw a rag doll lying in the sticks. It was grubby and alone.

John took Dicky by the hand and took him back to his family, who by this time were all packed up and ready to keep walking. John stood and watched them leave, before getting back on his horse. The road was now clear of all people, but he checked in both directions, before saying to Tony, "Follow me."

He led him down between the trees and through the curtain of thick growth on to the well-used track. He showed Tony the rag doll, who then alighted from his horse and put it in his saddle bag saying, "This doesn't belong here, I don't know about this track, but it could be the one we're searching for in this area. John, we can't be found on it, but we need to find out where it goes to the north."

"What do you want me to do Tony?"

"Return to Alex and tell him about it as quickly as possible, you found it, you go.'

"What are you going to do."

"Follow the track in a northerly direction, but not on it, I'll ride in the undergrowth within sight of it."

John rode back to where he knew Alex would be camped waiting for reports from the various undercover police. He had pushed his horse to arrive before nightfall. He was surprised to see Bill and Ian at the camp too, as well as Andy Willow.

"Where's Charley?" he asked as he alighted from his horse.

"A long way from here I hope," Bill replied

"Bill you have been eating sour fruit again!" John grinned at him and said.

The men laughed and Bill said, "John, I'll give you sour fruit in a minute if you're not careful!"

Alex looked at John's horse and asked, "Where's Tony?"

"We found a secret track and Tony's riding back in a northerly direction, keeping it in sight.'

"So that is why we couldn't find wheel tracks, well well…" Alex mused quietly.

"Beside the track, I found a rag doll and Tony put it in his saddle bag to show you. He said it didn't belong there," John added.

Both Ian and Bill were interested in the rag doll and John wondered why. They asked where it was found and was there anything in it?

"Nothing of note, just a dirty rag doll with some dried blood or something on it," John answered.

Andrew remained silent as this information was imparted.

"We'll have to map the track and watch it, noting any movement on it. I expect Tony will leave it at a point where he will be able to show us the extent of it," Alex said after the meal was eaten.

"If this is the track the man in question is using, he'll have men patrolling it, we can leave no evidence of our interest. On foot is the way we'll do it," Ian commented.

"Well armed too," Bill added.

"That goes without saying, these are dangerous men," Alex said, confirming Bill's words.

"Is Tony aware of the risks he's taking riding so close to it?" Ian asked John.

"I'm sure he does Ian, because a lot of the time Tony moves like a shadow in the bush, he can be quite unnerving.

The men talked into the night before they all retired and Bill said to John, "Remember no talking at breakfast."

John laughed and went to his swag saying, "Bill stop being a grump!"

Ian laughed and said, "Bill you asked for it!"

"I might have asked for it, but I didn't think he'd say anything in this company."

Within a short period there was silence in the camp and the normal nightlife was awake and on the move. In the morning John was the first man up and had the fire burning brightly. A billy was beginning to boil, he'd found the meat Andrew had brought from Green Hills, which was now sizzling on the fire. John stood up and looked at the sleeping forms and wondered how to wake them with the least damage to himself. A smile flashed across his face, as he unhobbled Bill's horse. He picked a bunch of green grass and put it near Bill's face, then he led his horse to the sleeping form. The horse was delighted and began to feed. The response was instant as Bill felt a big mouth on his mouth and let out a sudden cry.

"What the F--- is going on ?"

Everyone woke up instantly and John paid no attention sitting beside the fire, as Bill struggled to get out of the way of his horse, glaring at everyone for laughing. At last he turned to look at John sitting beside the fire.

"Good morning Bill, I trust you are a cheerful soul today," John said, looking up.

With everyone smiling Bill couldn't quite decide who was responsible for it.

"Whoever hobbled the horses last night did a poor job of it." Alex compounded the problem by saying.

No one said a word as they went for a wash in the creek and returned for a hearty breakfast.

"What do you want us to do today?" Ian asked Alex.

"Carry the news of the secret track back to Green Hills and send a note to Sergeant Green at Hill Top."

"Anything else?" Bill enquired.

"If you see Charley, pass it on please. I'll go with Andrew and John to find Tony. I think he must have had a bad night, we'll take him some food."

As the men saddled their horses, Bill walked across to John and put his arm across his shoulders tightly and said, "I will owe you one!"

"But Bill I remember you telling me the best way to wake up was to receive a kiss!"

"Not by a F—horse!" Bill said with a reluctant laugh.

"The horse is a mare, and a kiss is a kiss!"

"It is not John, take it from me!"

"No wonder you are so difficult in the mornings, you're never satisfied, just like today!"

John laughed and gave Bill a cheerful dig in the ribs saying, "Cheer up!"

"That was an interesting way to wake up." Ian said as he handed the reins to Bill.

"You wouldn't have liked feeling a horse eating grass on your face."

"Is that what it was doing?"

"You know it was, I saw you grinning."

"Bill, for an unusual wake up call, John was clever to pull it off so well. You have to give him credit, considering what he has had to endure from you in the last year."

"He's so easy to tease and takes it so well, so I do nothing?"

"You do nothing."

With the matter now settled Bill had the grace to laugh as he told his friend about John's words about the kiss! They rode away laughing.

Chapter 15

The long droving experience for Roy was an enjoyable one and while Mick knew he was a policeman the other men were ignorant of the fact. He was part of a team of men and was treated as an equal, and with his natural easy personality he fitted into the group very well. The nature of cattle was to wander in other directions as the mood took them and this kept the men busy during the days. At night it was a slow ride around the herd, keeping an eye out for trouble. They were fortunate that nothing caused the herd to panic, take fright and run, nor did anyone try and take a beast for food. Mick was satisfied with the price he was offered for the herd. He already had a figure in his head, given to him by Red Bryant, and the sale price was above it. Red would be pleased with the result.

The return journey took some days before Roy rode down the well-worn track to "River Oaks." Mick continued up to Red Bryant's farm, after he was told that Roy was to remain at "River Oaks".

Mr. and Mrs. Gill watched with interest and amusement at the continued courtship of Roy and Anne. There were good days and bad days when the whole household had a reason to go out on their horses.

"When you're courting don't bring her here until you have a definite answer, having Anne and Roy in the house, is like being at sea," Mr. Gill complained to his son Victor.

"What do you mean by saying it's like being at sea?"

"It isn't smooth sailing, nor is it comfortable with your sister's emotions all over the place."

Victor laughed and suggested, "I think Roy will be only too happy to go out with me for a few days. How long did Sergeant Green say he had to stay with us?"

"He didn't explain, except if Roy starts to withdraw into himself we have to send a message to him."

"Dad, do you know what is going on with the police?"

"No, I don't know. I do know we are keeping Roy occupied and busy for as long as we can, which is helping the police. That being said, take Roy out to a camp and let's have some peace in the house!"

The relief was quite likely felt by Mrs. Gill and her two daughters, Anne and Betty. Anne had had to endure comments from her brother, who at times found her behaviour exasperating, Victor thought Roy at times wasn't much better either and he wished they'd make up their minds about what they wanted to do.

As the summer progressed a change came over Roy, he slowly became quiet and was inclined to drift away from all of them in the house. Betty cornered him one morning in the stables.

"It's Steve isn't it that you're worried about now," she asked.

He folded up the saddle cloth and put it on the rack as Mr. Gill liked a tidy stable, turning to her replied, "Yes, I'm worried about him."

"Have you heard any word from him while you've been here."

"No, not since he left Red Bryant's property."

"So why are you worried about Steve?"

Roy wasn't comfortable, even though he was reasonably sure that Steve and Betty had an understanding

"Please tell me Roy," Betty asked again.

"I don't have to hear, I can feel when something is wrong."

Roy picked up the saddle and put it on the overhead rack, giving him time to think, because he couldn't tell Betty his exact feelings, as he wasn't entirely sure himself.

"I feel the time is approaching when Steve will need help from me," he said half to himself.

Betty wasn't happy and said, "I don't know how you can know that Roy."

Desperate to bring this conversation to an end Roy replied firmly, "I just do," then walked away to check on the horses.

Chapter 16

After John left, Tony rode his horse to the top of the next hill. He saw that the track was designed to take a dray and two horses. He sat still for a moment considering how clever it was, running all the time as far as possible parallel to the main track, which was used by ordinary people every day. He also noted that beams of wood had been put across deep gullies. Some of the gullies had been dug out to make it easy for the drays. Tony decided to return and follow the track towards the valley. He was aware of the need not to be seen, so at the top of each hill he cautiously alighted from his horse and looked down into the valley. If it was clear of any sign of life, he mounted his horse and continued to ride.

At the top of one hill he saw blue smoke rising from near a creek, and being late in the day it was almost certainly a night camp. It was time for him to leave the track and find a safe place to leave his horse. Tony found a good spot about a mile below the camp of the strange men. After unsaddling and hobbling his horse, he his swag near his saddle, took some dry rations and set off walking up the creek. Tony had learnt a number of useful lessons after his encounter with Ken and Steve. Keeping well out of sight was one of them. In this kind of work he'd learnt to move so quietly that the wildlife were not disturbed, they watched him, but didn't fly away and draw attention to his presence.

This time Tony decided to crawl as close to the camp as possible to listen. In these times men on the outer edge of the camp always listened to the wildlife around them. They were inclined to fire into the darkness, so Tony crawled as close as he dared.

"What news from the valley?" One of the men asked.

The man addressed grunted and asked, "First, is the track clear?"

"Yes, not a soul on it, we patrol it every day in both directions."

"Glad to hear it. There is news, a new fellah had a fight with Richards and killed him."

"How did they let that happen?"

"He needed to retire and Joe has taken over the lower valley."

"Who was the fellah who killed him?"

"A fighter called Steve, a dangerous man and Joe is planning to get rid of him as soon as he can find a good enough reason to do it."

"Why can't Joe just kill him?" Another voice asked.

"Steve's got friends in the valley. Joe has to find a reason whereby all his friends will stand by Joe."

"When can we return to the valley," another voice enquired.

"We're expecting a dray to come in late summer plus some important people. The track has to be patrolled until they leave."

"And if we see anyone?"

"They are to be killed as quietly as possible."

"Patrol it and keep it clear of trees and branches. Remember always quietly."

The men seemed to be aware that there was an unspoken threat in the words about being quiet, even Tony felt the sudden chill in the camp. He listened as the men prepared for the night and was suddenly quite still as a man walked to the edge of the camp, opened his fly, and relieved himself on Tony. This was a major drawback on this type of work! Once they were all asleep, he crawled back down the creek, a good way from the camp he stood and melted into the shadows. At his camp, and after a wash in the creek which included some of his clothes too, it was then into his swag.

Before sunrise Tony was up and wearing damp clothes, again no fire, no time to eat anything apart from dry rations, leading his horse through the undergrowth up to the normal track. With no traveller in sight, he stepped through the curtain of the bush, mounting his horse and rode towards Green Hills.

Tony hadn't ridden far when he saw his colleagues approaching. Winding their way down a steep hill towards a creek at the bottom of the incline. He found a good place to stop, he was tired, damp and wanted a mug of tea. This place was far enough away to be private from prying eyes. Tony alighted from his horse and before his friends arrived had a fire going, with a quart-pot on it. Alex rode up to the fire and dismounted and tied his horse to a tree, with Andrew and John following suit. Once they were all around the fire Tony repeated all he had heard from the men talking at the camp. He raised a laugh when he told them what he had endured on the edge of the camp. Tony had his tea and it was no surprise to his friends when he rolled over and went to asleep.

"You will remain here with Tony. Andrew, when you return to Green Hills, change into shabby clothes, change your horse and all police equipment to ordinary ones. Ride to tell Charley this news," Alex instructed.

"Do I stay with him?" John asked.

"Yes, continue to listen to men at the camps and John, be careful."

"What happens now," Andrew enquired.

"I'll return to Green Hills and send a message down to Sergeant Green," Alex replied.

"Do you know his role in this business?" Andrew asked quietly.

"Sergeant Green has an excellent intelligence network. I've been asked to keep him informed of all developments in this operation."

Chapter 17

Andrew Willow had been part of the Special Operation since early Spring and his job was carrying messages in his uniform. He never knew the contents, but at each delivery he was given a mug of tea and something to eat if it had been a long ride. More recently, after extra training, he'd begun to do undercover work on foot. This meant getting amongst travellers at night and listening to their conversation. In this way he'd collected more information about life in the valley, which was being investigated. Most of it filtered back to Sergeant Green, now he had a better idea after listening to Alex, not that Alex had told him very much at all, there were levels and levels in the police.

He'd been present when Ian and Bill had told Alex what they'd learnt from the city police about the lost children. Now there was a mystery surrounding Roy Cook and Steve Baker. None of the city police seemed to know about their training or anything concerning these two men. They seemed to be totally unknown, which was strange in a small police force.

Andrew had heard other bush police talk about how Fred Hall had been moved aside, to let Steve and Ken Taylor be trained for the undercover job. There was no talk about the best men for the job. He rode into the horse yard at his barracks, thinking his job was exciting, except for the dreary bits. It was only a short visit to make the change into shabby clothes. Walking out of his barracks towards the horse yards, he was pulled up by a yell.

"Hey you. Who the F—hell are you, and what were you doing in our barracks?"

Andrew thought, not that old bastard, he'll stop me for sure and I'm in a hurry to get out of here. He stopped walking as the old constable came striding towards him, with an irritated expression on his face.

"Miles you can't arrest me, you idiot!" Andrew said.

Instant recognition and Miles replied, "Yes I can, I can, I can arrest you on suspicion," then adding, "More undercover work?"

"Yes, the night camps."

"Better you than me."

"Your turn will come Miles"

"No it won't, I'm too well known in these parts."

Andrew was aware that Miles had some connections in the area of Green Hills, which put him under suspicion in the present time.

With this knowledge, Andrew replied, "More's the pity."

Miles glared at him saying, "What did you say Andy?"

"Nothing Miles."

Miles stood looking at him suspiciously, instinctively knowing there was a meaning behind his words. He could take exception if he'd understood him correctly, which he hadn't and this fact was irritating. Miles stood in front of his horse, as Andrew began to exit the police yard, saying, "What do you think you're going to do?"

"Work Miles, work."

"What if I told you to rake out the stables before going anywhere."

"You don't have that authority, it's your job Miles."

Miles grinned and said, "Andy you aren't going anywhere until you rake out the f—stables."

Miles closed the gate and ordered Andrew to dismount. He hadn't noticed Sergeant Shaw walking up behind him, as Miles stepped forward and pulled Andrew out of his saddle and gave him a good kick when he was on the ground. The Sergeant had heard stories about Miles being a bully to the younger constables, but he'd never actually witnessed Miles Wells in action before today.

"Why are you on the ground." he asked Andrew as if he had just arrived at this scene.

Miles answered for him, "He fell off his horse."

Andrew stood up, dusted himself down and stood by his horse.

"He has to rake out the stables before going to play at being undercover policeman," Miles, feeling on safe ground, explained to the Sergeant.

The Sergeant had other ideas and said mildly, "No Mr. Wells, you will be cleaning out the stables, it is your job. I'll come and inspect your work."

Miles Wells looked shocked and said without thinking, "I'm not F__ doing that job, it's for the young bastards like this one here to do it."

The Sergeant had been trying to find a reason to get rid of this lazy constable, ever since suspicion had arisen about his loyalty to his station in this Special Operation. Now he'd crossed the line of no return and again the Sergeant spoke quietly, "Mr. Wells, you will do the escort to the city tomorrow morning, and take your swag with you, you will not be returning here. That is all, except rake out the stables now, if you please."

Miles muttering under his breath walked into the stables and Andrew heard something being thrown hard at the wall.

"Mr. Willow you may leave now and please give Mr. Rush my best wishes when you see him," his Sergeant said mildly.

"Yes Sergeant I will, thank you."

The Sergeant pattered the rump of Andrew's horse as he rode through the gateway. At the stable doorway Andrew saw Miles with an outraged expression on his face, and he heard his Sergeant say, "Get on with raking out the stable Mr. Wells, I'll stay and keep you company, while you work."

Andrew smiled and when he was out of sight of the settlement, laughed as he rode in a northerly direction. Once he reached the area of interest, he took his horse to a squatter who helped the police, when they needed assistance. He was only too happy to look after Andrew's horse. Andrew's work was on foot and there was no way a shabbily dressed individual could own a horse if he was honest.

It was not the easiest job to find Charley, because he was unable to ask if anyone had seen him. He walked in several directions over the next couple of days with no sign of him. At last walking down a little used track he saw Charley at a fire, smelling meat cooking, which was a relief because his rations were almost non-existent.

Charley looked up at Andrew and said grudgingly, "F-hell, now I've got to share it!"

Not in the least put out by these words Andrew laughed and said, "Yes, Charley and I'm hungry."

"Can't you be F—hungry elsewhere?"

"No, I can just taste that juicy meat by it's scent."

"F—hell, Andy what are you doing out here?"

"Looking for you."

"Can't you go away and come back in a couple of hours' time!"

"No Charley, not with the scent of that lovely meat in my mouth."

"Oh! Well, perhaps you can have the leftovers!"

"No Charley, I'm younger than you are and I need building up, at your age you don't need as much food!"

Charley laughed and clouted Andrew for good measure before handing him a slice of meat. He was actually pleased to have the young bush policeman at his camp. He was a cheerful companion, not like Bill Todd who was painful to endure for more than two minutes.

"How did you get such a good meal?" Andrew asked.

"Playing cards. He was no F—good at them, and it was easy to get the meat before some other bastard beat me to it," Charley grinned.

"I'm going to enjoy working with you Charley, whatever you do don't lose your touch!" Andrew said cheerfully.

"I won't Andy, so what's the news?"

Andrew told him all about Miles Wells and Charley said, "He was a right bastard and you won't see him again.'

Charley was intrigued about the missing children and in relation to Steve Baker and Roy Cook. He was from the city and this was news. His territory now being played out in the bush, was basically a city problem. The other news about the secret track and what Tony had heard, caused Charley to do some deep thinking. He'd kept quiet as Andrew told him all that he'd been asked to pass on, plus some observations. In the silence at the end of the flow of words, Andrew waited for a response.

"Well… well," Charley said.

"Is that all you can say?"

Charley replied slowly, "I'm thinking Andrew, I'm thinking."

"What are you thinking?"

"I'm thinking Andrew, something in the valley is coming to a head and we have to find out what's brewing? We need to be in the camps at night where the men are talking."

"Are we going now?"

"Andy, don't be so F—impatient, we have to work out how to get information back to Alex in a hurry, if we hear it."

"My horse is with a friendly squatter near here."

This was news to Charley who suddenly looked a lot happier.

"Is it now?" he said.

"Yes, near here."

"Right, we work together, me on one side of a group and you on the other side, anyone who mentions the name of Joe, note it."

"Okay, we'd better be going Charley and you can chew that bone as we walk!"

"And you can chew the other F—one too!"

"I will be delighted to do so in such exalted company!"

"Andy, you'll get a clip on the ear in a moment, if you're not F—careful"

Andrew laughed as they walked up the path chewing their bones, heading for the main track over the hill. They both had a pouch for rations and none of the luxuries like soap. After finishing the bones, they wiped greasy hands on their trousers. A wash using mud cleaned the hands when the opportunity arose and they were close to water. Being out on track, they took care of their few possessions, fully aware of their light-fingered neighbours, as they listened to the local gossip. Most of it was useless but sometimes small 'nuggets of gold' were to be noted.

It didn't take them long to be aware something was seriously brewing in the valley. It was that certain intangible feeling of discord in the air, a type of fear, shown in quiet voices. Charley put it down to the fact of the man in question coming to his valley. Men and women were mortally afraid of him and his cruelty.

Charley was shocked when Andrew commented, "Joe is in the valley, why are you concerned about a man coming to the valley?"

Charley proceeded to fill in the details of the overall picture.

"So that's what this is all about, Joe is the key for Steve and Ken to get out before that man arrives in the valley." Andrew responded.

"Yes Andy, if they can escape, that is"

"Did I tell you all that information from Alex?"

"You did Andy and you told it very well."

"That's what all those odd messages meant?'

"Yes Andy."

"To quote you Charley. Well….Well."

Each morning Charley and Andrew, ragged, dirty and unshaven, mingled with equally unkempt men in the groups, this being the safe way to walk from place to place. Several days passed with the groups of men unaware that two of their party never really left the area, joining at night and vanishing during the day until Andrew drew Charley's attention to a group of men.

"One of these men rescued Steve and Ken from us," he said.

"Andy get as close as you can to them tonight and I will too."

The talk was quite loud and everyone heard it as one of the men talked of friction in the valley. Joe had at last found a way to deal with Steve, who was a nasty piece of work, it'd be a good fight.

"How's he going to do it?" Another man asked.

There was an answer in a soft voice.

"Speak up, we didn't hear you," Another man said

"He said it was something to do with the F—police."

"What is?"

"That bastard Steve is to be accused of being an undercover policeman, he'll have no friends now to support him."

"But if it isn't true?"

"No matter, he'll be doomed and Joe will win the fight."

Andrew crawled away into the undergrowth, meeting Charley who had also heard the fateful words. Both men crept away from the camp for a reasonable distance before standing up.

"Andy, can you find your squatter in the moonlight?" Charley whispered.

"Yes, I can find him."

"Good, go quickly to Alex, wake him up and tell what we've heard."

"Anything else?"

"Yes Ride down to Hill Top and pass the information on to Sergeant Green, do you know your way to that settlement?"

"Yes Charley, I've been there lots of times carrying messages."

"Good lad, off you go"

"What about you Charley?"

"I'm alright, I'll come home in my own time. Now go."

"Don't play cards and win meat, if I'm not here to help you eat it!" Andy said quietly before walking away.

Before Charley could respond Andrew had melted into the shadows, leaving a grinning friend staring into the darkness.

Chapter 18

Mr. Gill decided it was time to talk to Roy about the instructions he'd had from Sergeant Green some months ago, when Roy had been on the cattle drive south.

"Sergeant Green requested that I was to teach you about being a Squatter. I will say you're a quick learner soaking up everything you've been taught here.

"I do appreciate all you've taught me and I've enjoyed the work," Roy said.

"Sergeant Green also told me that there would become a time when you will need to leave here. He explained that you and Steve are close and you know when he's in trouble?"

"Yes I do Mr. Gill, and I'm not happy because Steve is worried about something."

"I think it's time for you to go to Hill Top and talk to Sergeant Green. He's a man with a deep understanding of your gift, he has two cousins like you. He's grown up seeing this gift used in ways which defy reasonable explanations. Steve had a talk to him before leaving to travel north."

"It's just like Steve to tell Sergeant Green, without asking me first, if I wanted him to know."

"Roy, when you get to Hill Top you won't have to explain your gift to the sergeant. Steve has prepared him and he'll know how to help you," then added after a moment's silence, "Roy you can leave in the morning early, that's the best time to ride."

Roy seemed hesitant about something and, Mr. Gill, knowing what was in his mind, smiled and said, "You leave Anne to me, just come back in one piece!"

Roy's face changed colour as he said, "She isn't easy."

"I know that. I'm her Father!"

They walked back along the bank of the creek to the house. Roy went to the room he shared with Victor and prepared his swag, with his few possessions. In this quiet time in the late afternoon, he felt Steve was safe just now, but something was coming to a head. Steve would need him to be somewhere, but as yet he couldn't see where this was to be. Roy knew when he would need to know, the knowledge would be in his head. Roy smiled as he thought as policemen this knowledge was never evidence, it had to be found.

They'd had a talk before Steve left to go away.

"Neither Betty nor Anne are going to like being separated, any more than we like being apart for long periods," he'd said.

Roy had filed these words away in his mind, but he remembered them now. He thought when Steve was safe they could talk about their future. Closing his swag these words vanished from his mind, as Anne came flooding into it. She wasn't going to be happy to hear he was going away for a considerable amount of time. He waited until after the evening meal to talk to her.

Roy was partially relieved when Mr. Gill announced at the end of the meal, "Roy will be leaving in the morning, to ride up to Hill Top on a police Operation."

There were questions and answers around the table, and a total silence from Anne, who obviously wasn't happy at this announcement by her Father. This didn't bode well for Roy when he and Anne met later.

It was essential in the bush that everything possible had to be made, and sewing was part of the life of women. Rooms for privacy at "River Oaks" were in a short supply, so Anne chose the sewing room at the end of the verandah to talk with Roy.

This meeting progressed well until Anne couldn't hold back her jealousy over Roy's concern for Steve, putting him first instead of her well-being.

"When Betty had her accident from her horse, you knew about it and went to her aid, almost without thinking, didn't you?" Roy said, trying to explain.

"That's different we're twins"

"Steve and I are like that in all but name."

"You aren't twins, so it isn't the same."

Roy being fed up with his dearly beloved replied without thinking.

"Anne, don't be silly, of course it's the same as twins."

Her expression turned to outrage and she replied in a brittle voice, "So I'm silly, am I?"

Roy, instead of making a soothing reply, made a thoughtless one.

"Yes, when you refuse to face a truth like this one."

Anne, red in the face rose out of her chair and glared at Roy and flounced out of the small room in a grand huff, with tears beginning to spill from her eyes. Roy made no effort to stop her, feeling totally at sea. He sighed and left the room to meet Betty on the short verandah, who didn't appear to be her normal cheerful self.

"What's up?" Roy asked.

He's younger than Steve, Betty thought, and one day will make a good husband for Anne, once Steve is safe.

"Roy, write a letter to Anne and explain again about your relationship with Steve. Don't try and compare you and Steve to twins, you and Steve will always be a unit, as long as you live. Leave it in your room after you leave, Victor will give it to her in the morning," she suggested.

"Do you want me to deliver a letter to Steve?" Roy asked.

"Yes, I've written a letter for you to give to him."

"He'll love to get a letter from you, Betty"

"Do you think so?"

"Of course he will."

"You are so sure Roy."

"I'm not only sure Betty, but I also know he lives with a hope in his heart."

With these words Betty wished Roy a good night and a safe journey.

He went to his room and was relieved to see that Victor had not yet retired. He composed a letter to Anne which was completed by the time he heard Victor's boots coming along the wooden floor outside their room.

In the morning, before sunrise, Roy was at the stable saddling his police horse with the police equipment which had been kept out of sight during his stay at "River Oaks."

It was also months since he'd worn his uniform and it had a good feeling to be going back on the job, except he had a long way to go to get his other half back to safety.

He was strapping on his lightly packed swag, as Victor walked into the yard saying, "I thought I heard you moving early, bumping into that table, loud enough to wake up anyone!"

"Victor, it wasn't that loud."

Victor laughed and asked, "Would you like some company for half a day?"

"Yes, for a couple of hours it would be nice, thanks."

Victor saddled one of the horses in the yard and Roy commented, "The horses aren't usually in the yard over night?"

"No, I put mine in last night, you didn't expect me to run around the paddock at this hour did you Roy?"

He laughed and replied, "No, probably not."

They rode out of the yard and down the road to the front track which passed the Gill's land before turning north.

"We can stop at Red's place for a mug of tea and I'll ride home from there or stay the night and leave early in the morning," Victor suggested.

"I'll stop for a mug of tea and then keep going Victor. I'm sure trouble is coming to Steve and I can't stop until I get to Hill Top."

They rode in silence until Victor said, "I heard you had a difficult talk with Anne last night."

"Yes, I love her but Steve's like my brother and he's in trouble now."

"We all know you love Steve as well as Anne, she'll come round in the end, she always does, you know."

"I hope so."

"I've decided that I expect to have you and Steve as brother's-in-law, so don't go changing your mind or there really will be trouble!"

It was just as well for Roy that he didn't know that Anne was awake when he rode out of the yard with Victor. Why wasn't she riding with him instead of her brother? Fresh tears fell onto her pillow.

CHAPTER 19

Dommy was disturbed at the gossip he was hearing in the hut where the men camped. It was even worse at the meal tables where he served every day. This kind of talk seemed to be attractive to the men, when the work was slowing down and they easily became bored. A bit of cruelty went a long way to making them settle and become ordinary human beings. Ordinary for the valley perhaps, but nowhere else. Joe was forever talking about Steve and how he distrusted him. In recent weeks Joe was now suggesting that Steve would be better if he were no longer alive. It was eating at Joe that he had men who liked Steve, it had to change. In one hut Dommy overheard a conversation between Joe and his close mates.

"What have you come up with Freddy?" Joe had asked quietly.

"We could spread it around that they were undercover police, men would drop away from them like flies from a dry bone."

"Let's do it for a couple weeks and then strike Ken, he'll go straight to the ants to give the men some sport and I'll get to kill the big bastard."

Dommy waited until all the men had gone to their bunks and silence reigned except for the multitude of snoring breaking the still night. This sound covered his departure, as he walked quickly and carefully in the moonlight down to Kevin's hut. Kevin was a light sleeper and heard footsteps approaching his doorway and moved silently out his door. Steve was accustomed to Kevin going outside during the night and closed his eyes again. On this night Kevin was out longer than usual, Steve left his bunk and went outside to see Dommy and Kevin talking. Both men looked up at his approach as they were out of the moonlight in the shade of a tree. Kevin beckoned Steve into the shade saying

"We can't be seen here and I expected you sooner."

A few minutes later Ken came out of the hut and joined Steve in the darkness, waiting to be told what this gathering meant. Dommy was clearly nervous, he left and was soon swallowed up in the night.

"We need to talk as there's been a development which we can't ignore." Kevin said.

"What is it?" Ken asked.

Kevin explained, telling his two friends all that Dommy had told him a few minutes before. Steve began to say something, Kevin held up his hand saying, "Stop, I have to tell you something."

He smiled and began to speak, "I've always known you are both undercover policemen since you arrived when you Ken were delirious and talked clearly. I've kept quiet because this valley needs a new beginning. This is no longer an issue, planning your escape is important."

Steve looked at Kevin's face, lined with age and asked, "If you help us will harm come to you?"

Even in the night light Kevin's face seemed to smooth as he absorbed those words and replied, "Isn't it like you Steve to ask a question like that one, when your lives hang in the balance. I can look after myself. If we play our cards right no one will know of my part in your escape."

"Did I say very much in that delirium?" Ken asked.

"Enough to get you hanged!" Kevin grinned.

"Thank you for our lives Kevin."

"Don't think about, I've enjoyed your company. It's a long time since I spent hours in the company of men who want to make a difference in this crooked world. You were always safe with me."

There was silence and nothing moved in the moonlight which showed that it was safe to talk, so Kevin explained his plan for their escape.

"Everyone is accustomed to seeing you both with the cows, when the time is right, you will drive them down to the creek. I'd suggest you take them there tomorrow and look at where the water drops under the hill. I made the same trip when I was a young man."

"How much warning will we have, do think?" Steve asked.

"As soon as Dommy says the word it's instant departure from here. Tonight we'll discuss the plan in detail, from now onwards you'll always carry whatever you may need on that journey."

"In time to come Ken and I will do our best for you, Dommy and a couple of other men, but we are unable to promise anything." Steve said softly.

"I knew you'd say something like that, I'll appreciate just living in this valley as a free man, but the law might not see it like that, considering my past years?' Kevin replied.

They all returned to the hut for the remainder of the night, after all, the cows had to be milked in the morning.

Chapter 20

If the walls of "River Oaks" were a sentient being it would've enjoyed the recent summer. As it was, Betty, Anne, Victor and Roy heard lots of conversations between Eva and Alan Gill, which had been thought to be private. The walls of the slab huts had cracks and sounds carried far beyond the quietly spoken word. There were talks about Roy, which was an ongoing subject, a handsome man who was a policeman. Why was he here? Victor heard his parents talking about Roy the night before he left.

"What do I say to him?" Alan had asked Eva.

"Keep it simple Alan, talk about Sergeant Green."

"Do I mention we have been in communication with him."

"No, talk about our daughter Anne if you have to talk, after all we don't know if these two men will survive the coming encounter."

Victor smiled as he rode beside Roy and thought about the recent summer concerning the man he was riding beside now.

During the Summer Red Bryant received a letter from his distant neighbours, Alan and Eva Gill, expressing their concern about what kind of man Roy Cook was? They requested assurance that he was of good character because he was courting their daughter Anne. In the letter it was clear they didn't understand Roy's relationship with Steve Baker. Red had been expecting a communication of some kind from Alan Gill on this subject, considering Alan's earlier experience with two stockmen he had employed for two years. Red thought about their letter and decided to send it to Sergeant Green, who in turn wrote an understanding reply to Alan and Eva Gill, assuring them that Roy was quite normal but with an unusual gift.

Sergeant Green also wrote a second letter to Red requesting him to make a visit to "River Oaks". In the letter Alan and Eva had written, was the information that their son Victor was sharing his room with Roy. The Sergeant made several requests to Red, which he wanted passed on to Victor, so it was with considerable interest when Alan made an announcement at the meal table one night.

"We're expecting a visit from our distant northern neighbour, Red Bryant, in the next day or so."

"Is Mr Bryant staying the night?" Eva asked.

"Yes, he'll be staying a couple of nights."

"What's he coming down here for Dad?" Victor had asked.

"To look at our cattle," adding, "I want you to take him out to see the cattle in the area at the foot of the hills."

"Do you know if the two blocks of land between us and Mr. Bryant have been assigned yet?" Betty asked her father.

"The word is that the two land blocks are in reserve."

"Have you heard who our new neighbours are to be Dad?" Anne asked.

"No, I don't know yet, I did enquire and was informed I'd be told in time."

"Can we continue to run our cattle on those areas Dad?" Victor enquired.

"Yes, we can. I was told that the new owners won't be taking up their land until well into autumn or winter."

•

Red Bryant rode into the horse yard at "River Oaks" late the next afternoon, cheerfully greeting the Gill family as they came out of various doors to greet him. He handed over a package which his wife Mary had sent down for the girls. It was soon unwrapped, and the contents vanished into their room, with words and laughter.

The next day Victor took Red out to see the cattle and was surprised when Red chose a shaded place near water and dismounted.

"Make a fire and we'll have a mug of tea, talking is thirsty work," he said.

"Don't you want to look at the cattle?" Victor asked, standing beside his horse.

"No, I've come down here to talk to you. Now make that fire."

Victor tied his horse to a tree, made the fire, then walked to the water and filled two quart-pots and put them amongst the hot coals in the fire. Red was already seated leaning against a log. Victor sat opposite him and listened with interest as Red revealed the contents of the two letters. He explained who they had been sent to and why he was now at "River Oaks." Regardless of the walls, Victor decided this was all news to him.

"I didn't want to share my room with Roy after my earlier experience with Steve Baker, who I discovered was a very dangerous man," he said.

Red asked for an explanation and Victor told him.

Red was inclined to treat it as a joke and asked, "Did Steve really creep up to you and you never heard him approach?"

"Yes, he did, and I get the shivers just thinking about it."

"Victor, you're bush trained, I know you can move silently, that Steve, who is a city boy to all intents and purposes can beat you, he'd have to be very good."

"He was very good; I can still feel his hands around my neck."

Red was clearly impressed and remained quiet for a while.

"Roy isn't as dangerous as Steve, though he has other abilities," he said.

"Is Roy a normal man like you and me?" Victor enquired carefully.

"You shared a room with him, don't you know?"

"I know, but I'm uneasy."

"Yes, Roy is quite normal, why would you think otherwise?"

"The way he talks about Steve, it's as if he loved him."

"Victor, he does love Steve, just the same way as Betty loves Anne."

"So it's that way."

"Yes Victor, it's the normal way. Did you think otherwise or what's on your mind?"

"I don't know, I just don't understand Roy."

Red laughed with real humour and replied, "Roy has an unusual gift, he always knows when Steve is in trouble or if his life's threatened. Just like Anne and Betty know things about each other without being told.'

"What you're saying is that they're normal men, with the same needs as we do at times."

"Yes, Steve told me they sorted this aspect out when they were young men, before joining the police. They know each other's strengths and weaknesses. Roy has the strongest mind and Steve the greatest depth. They are both strong and as you say, Steve can be lethal."

Victor stirred the coals with a stick, before asking quietly, "What do you want from me? Roy has bad dreams. I often hear him muttering in his sleep and a few times I've had to wake him. He thinks I'm Steve, which I've found disturbing."

"Explain please."

"He'll take hold of me in an embrace or hug for a moment, then say he's sorry. He thought I was Steve."

"Do you ever ask what caused the bad dream?"

"Only once and his face turned white, and he said meat ants."

"What did you make of that answer?"

"Nothing and on that occasion he'd put his arms around me, and I didn't like it, so I told him not to be silly."

Red continued to examine Victor's understanding, by asking, "What happened then?"

"He went quiet and eventually went back to sleep, I wondered what he'd seen."

"I can answer that question for you. In the closed valley where Steve and Ken are at the present time, this is how men are killed, an agonizing death, being eaten alive. Roy sees what Steve is seeing."

A shocked expression flashed across Victor's face as he slowly digested these terrible words. He sat looking into the fire stunned at the sheer cruelty, remembering what he had said to Roy.

"Only men?" He asked quietly.

Red answered equally quietly. "No Victor......We only know the gossip talked around the campfires at night. We don't know exactly what's happening in the valley."

They talked quietly and Red made some requests concerning Roy's bad dreams.

"I want you to record any clear words Roy says in his dreams, don't try and seek their meanings. Leave that job to Sergeant Green. Send the material to me and I'll forward it on to the Sergeant," he said.

Victor stirred the coals sending up a shower of sparks and Red commented, "Just as well it rained last night and the grass is wet."

"Or my father would skin me alive if I started a fire!" Victor grinned, adding "What would it be like to have a brother or a friend like Roy? I like my privacy."

"I don't know, they've grown up together and they are melded to each other. Steve once told me they do have private thoughts, which they don't talk about. Being aware is sufficient to each other."

Victor used the remaining water in his quart-pot to put out the fire and standing up looking down at Red asked, "How do they cope with each other being in love with my sisters."

Red stood and laughing said, "I don't know, except they could never marry any other than twins, who are as close as your sisters. The big question will be how your sisters will cope with Roy and Steve?"

"When you put it in those terms, I'd say stormy weather is approaching!"

Red mused as he put his quart-pot into its leather bag attached to his saddle.

"The whole four of them will have to meld together to make it work well, if it is going to work at all."

Victor mounted and asked, "Anything else on your agenda for me to do?"

"Yes, when the time comes, I want you to ride up to my place with Roy, he can't travel on his own but give me some warning beforehand if you can so I can get a message to Sergeant Green."

CHAPTER 21

As Roy caught sight of the turn-off to Red's place, he turned to his companion saying, "Victor, you've been away in a daydream for ages, it must've been a good one, do you want to share any of it?"

"No Roy I've thinking about summer and all the work we've achieved having help," Victor laughed.

"That's kind of you to say when I have a great deal to learn. I've enjoyed the days too, but not the nights, Steve thinks about things before he goes to sleep."

Turning down the well-worn road to Red's horse yards. Roy was surprised to see two police horses tied up to the hitching rail under the tree. Red saw them arrive in the late morning and came out to greet Victor and Roy saying, "Come in, you're just in time for a meal."

Victor alighted and tied his horse to the rail, while Roy still sat in his saddle.

"Come on Roy, you can have a quick meal and be on your way again," Victor looked up and said.

He alighted and after checking on his horse, followed Victor into Red's abode, greeted Mary and nodded to Ian Percy. He'd met Ian when Steve had arrived here in the early spring. James Wade was a new face, and Roy was only too happy to talk to him across the table. Ian indicated to Victor that he thought one of his horse's shoes might be coming adrift and that this was a good time to go out and check.

Roy heard and began to get up and Mary said firmly, "No Roy, not until you have eaten a good meal, Victor and Ian are quite capable of checking the horse's shoe on their own."

He sat down again and asked James what had been happening in his world.

Meanwhile Ian led Victor across the yard to where the horses were tied up and moved to one side, out of view of Red's home.

"Any sign yet of where Roy is to meet Steve?" Ian turned to Victor and asked

"So that's why you wanted me to come outside with you?'

"Yes, we'll accompany Roy up to Hill Top, as yet we have no idea how Steve and Ken will escape that valley."

"Can't you just ask him straight out?" Victor asked.

"No, his knowledge doesn't operate that way. Steve told us it comes out during the night, if it's important, he'll remember it and talk about it."

"So that's why he has to have a companion all the time now, does Roy know of this development?"

"On one level yes, on another probably not, he has always taken care of Steve, as Steve has taken care of him, but this is something new, right outside of their experience."

"I thought you worked with Bill Todd?" Victor curiously asked.

"I do, but we have to know where Roy will meet Steve, once we do James will ride to Green Hills as fast as possible."

"You are well organized."

Ian laughed in a strange way indicating uncertainty and replied, "I do hope so Victor, I do hope so."

They walked back into the cheerful room and Roy asked, "How was the horseshoe?"

"Not as bad as I'd thought," Ian replied

Roy smiled and Victor thought he knows it wasn't the fantasy of the horseshoe; it was to talk about him. Victor at last understood, and before he left for home he had a few words with Roy

"I'm sorry," he said.

"Don't be Victor, it will end soon and Steve and I will be free."

Within a short time after Victor had gone, Roy, accompanied by Ian and James, continued riding north. They made camp in the late afternoon, beside a small flowing creek. This setting was familiar to Ian who said, looking around the area, "I've been here before in early spring."

"Most creeks look the same to me, it's the hills which are different," James commented.

Ian took a fishing line out of his saddlebag and walked up the banks of the creek. This was a quiet place to think, as he searched for a deep hole and a fish. James was quite contented to make the fire and cook the meat Mary Bryant had given at their departure. Roy sat by the fire after filling the quart-pots.

"I hear you are having a difficult few days," James asked him.

"I'm waiting to get a message."

"Don't worry about it, when it comes, it will be clear, that's what my Mum says."

"I just wish it would come," Roy grinned and replied.

"It will come when it's least expected and then we can act accordingly."

Ian returned without any fish saying, "I need Bill to catch fish."

"Bill told me not to rely on you to get any food out of the water!" James laughed and explained.

"He did, did he"

"Yes, he said you were a good swimmer but were unable to catch anything else with the same ability."

Ian said in an irritated tone of voice, "Well, why don't you get off your backside and go and catch a bloody fish."

"Why bother when we have meat."

There was silence as they glared at each other for a moment or two. Roy didn't seem to be aware of either man as he gazed into the fire. His very stillness caused Ian and James to forget their conflict and look at him, as he began to speak slowly.

"Steve and Ken have been shown a way out of the valley, their departure is imminent, just waiting…"

Another silence and Roy continued, "Water, they will be in water, they can't leave the water."

Ian didn't say a word for a few minutes, as Roy lapsed back into silence. Then he spoke, "Wherever possible the area around the valley was mapped, at a distance from the hills, it was noted that a stream of water came out of an underground cave. Within a short distance the stream flowed into a river. This river meanders out into the open plain."

Roy spoke again slowly, "I have to meet Steve and Ken on that river at a place I can't quite see yet."

"Is it a long way out on the plain?" Ian asked.

"Yes, it is. You know where it is." Roy replied in an irritated voice.

"How can I know?"

"You were there with Bill and another policeman."

"How do you know Roy?"

"I see shadows there, it is opposite….. I can't quite see it."

"Keep trying Roy, don't give up, concentrate, opposite what?"

"It's totally dead, very strange."

"Dead what?"

"Water."

Ian remembering what the Old Man had told him and Bill, asked, "How dead?"

"Something ancient is sleeping in the depth of the water, I can't see it's form, only aware it has been sleeping for centuries."

Ian explained to James, "It's a dead waterhole where no animals or birds go to drink, the water is black and there was an eerie feeling near it."

"It's opposite this place that we must make camp and wait," Roy stated clearly.

Roy ate his meat and fell asleep almost immediately in his swag, while Ian had removed pen and ink from his saddlebag and wrote a report. In the fading light, he completed it and folding the paper handed it to James.

"You'll leave here at dawn and ride as fast as it's safe to do so, taking care of your horse. Deliver this note to Sergeant Green. He'll give you another note to be delivered to Alex Pitt or if you can't find him Charley Rush," he said.

"Do you want me to return to you after I've made these deliveries?"

"No, ask Sergeant Green what he needs you to do before riding north with the papers."

That night Roy slept without any bad dreams and Ian let him sleep until he awoke naturally, well after sunrise in the early morning. James had left at early dawn, riding away in the moonlight.

Roy and Ian had a last mug of tea before departing for Hill Top. Roy was silent as if he'd been drained of words, just gazing into the fire and watched Ian pour a quart-pot of water onto it. The red coals turned black as the hot steam rose into the air, as he left the fire, put his swag and quart-pot on his horse and mounted. They rode in silence until the late afternoon, when Ian suggested, "Do you want a rest?'

"No thanks Ian, we keep going."

They made camp in a quiet place eating the last of the meat given by Mary, and in the morning, Roy asked, "When do you think James will reach Hill Top?"

"I'd think early today. Are you concerned about Steve and Ken?"

"No, not now. Steve loves a challenge and seems quite contented; he and Ken make a good pair."

"You don't often speak about Ken," Ian said.

"Ken is a quiet kind of man who grew up on a farm, he takes what comes in his stride dealing with one problem at a time. Steve and Ken will never let harm come to each other; they are firmly united."

"They are good friends?"

"Yes definitely," adding, "They'll be friends for life after this experience."

It was a long day's ride well into twilight when they rode into the police barracks horse yard at Hill Top. Ian was pleased to be met by the farrier who told both men, "I'll see to your horses, take your gear, the Sergeant wants to see you the moment you arrive here."

They thanked him and carrying their swags walked up to his office situated at the end of the wooden slabbed barracks, dropping the swags outside his door, they knocked and entered.

Sergeant Green greeted both men as they walked into his small domain. He indicated they could sit on the smooth-topped stumps near his desk and enquired about their trip

"Mr. Wade arrived here early this morning, I read your report Mr. Percy and made some additions. He is now on his way to Green Hills. Mr. Cook, when you have had your evening meal come back here. Mr. Percy I'd like to see you here in the morning with details about the place on the river opposite the dead waterhole," he informed them.

"Yes, Sergeant I'll work on it tonight."

"All your particular friends are away at the present time, so I daresay there will be no one coming tomorrow to complain?" The Sergeant smiled and said.

"I may not have the time to examine that particular tent tonight," Ian smiled and replied carefully.

"If you do, try not to commit too much trouble for me!"

"I'll keep your words in mind Sergeant."

The men left the office and Roy asked, "What was the Sergeant talking about?"

Ian laughed and replied cheerfully, "We visit a certain tent in the settlement and after a few drinks there are young girls employed to entertain us and it's fun. An old man usually complains."

"Steve and I use to enjoy places like that, until we met Anne and Betty."

The meal shed was almost empty with a couple of older constables sitting hunched over the bench in the corner. They ate the meat with fresh damper, talking quietly together until the end of their repast, then Ian went to do his report and Roy walked down to the office.

He knocked and entered. They spoke of general activities and Roy's gift of knowledge.

"Are you confident Mr. Baker and Mr. Taylor can escape from the valley unharmed?" Sergeant Green asked.

"Steve can block me out when he doesn't want me to know some of his activities, we do it to each other. He has put up a block, so I've no idea how he and Ken will escape from the valley." Roy replied in a resigned tone of voice, adding after thinking for a moment or two, "If they make the escape, the place I've indicated is where they will end up. It won't be for some days; how many I don't know."

"What do you know Mr. Cook?"

"If they get that far they will be in a poor condition and need good food and clothes."

"So you are not certain of their escape?"

"No Sergeant, but I know Steve and Ken. I know they are two powerful men, if anyone can make that escape, they will do it."

"Okay Mr. Cook, I will send Mr. Percy with two other police and yourself out to that place on the river. In two days you will leave here with two extra horses and two pack horses. Mr. Percy will be in charge with you as his advisor."

In the morning Ian walked to the office a little unsteadily and was greeted by his Sergeant with a joyful expression saying, "Just the man I want to see, the Minster from the local meeting house has a new bell and wants a hand to put it up, I've volunteered you to help him."

Ian inwardly groaned and wished he'd refrained from all that beer last night but not the girl that went with it, as he went in search of the Minister. The man didn't know anything about a bell and Ian had a lot to say under his breath about his Sergeant! The settlement wasn't the best place to wander about in the early mornings as some people didn't look where they were emptying nightsoil. Ian was almost hit by one lot, and let the individual know what would've happened to him, had it landed on even his boot.

"He's a F— sour bastard," he heard as he walked away.

Ian smiled and took a short cut to his barracks for a mug of tea before going to the Sergeant's office. He knocked and entered, the man looked up from a pile of papers and said, "Enjoy the walk?'

"Yes, I did, and the Minister is looking forward to seeing you in his congregation next Sunday."

Ian saw the sudden expression on his Sergeant's face which made it all worthwhile. Not for a moment did Ian show any humour, but deep down he was delighted. Ian thought he'd be a long way away, when his Sergeant found out that the Minister was creating new members of his tiny community on the next Sunday.

Not by the smallest touch of humour did the Sergeant indicate his thoughts, but he was equally pleased and replied, "I shall look forward to greeting the Minster."

"The men from the valley will do their utmost to capture Mr. Taylor and Mr. Baker, you will not let them take these men under any circumstances. As many other police from other areas as can be spared, will be sent to you. I've sent a note to Mr. Todd." He said, moving some papers and looking up.

"When do we leave here?'

"In two days', time."

CHAPTER 22

Ken and Steve woke up as usual before sunrise, Kevin, who was already out of his bunk, talked about when he was a young man when he and a friend decided to explore the cave. It took courage to go down into the water, where it dropped out of sight.

"We were young and immortal or so we thought at the time, we were strong swimmers and dived into the water," he told them. "The stream split and I took the left-hand side, and my friend took the other side and was never seen again," he added.

"How far were you below the water level?" Steve asked.

"Only in short places where the cave roof was low, pretty much the same as the water is on the outside now."

"How long were you under the water, and are they long caves?" Ken enquired.

"That's hard to remember, I do think it felt that it would never come to an end."

"Please Kevin, try to remember."

"It was a long time ago Ken, there are air pockets throughout the cave system. It's vital that you both remain in the central current all the time. At either end there will be a twilight, a darkness of various types elsewhere."

"Is there anything else you can tell us, Kevin?" Steve asked.

"You have to remember I'm talking about a memory of twenty years ago, there have been floods in those years. It could have changed, and some rocks have sharp edges, so keep all your clothes on, including boots."

"How do we stay together in the caves?" Ken asked thoughtfully.

"This is important, I will put a rope on one of the cows after the milking has been completed. You will have to decide how you will be tied, and the rope will be in place for many days. You have a long way to go. When you sleep Ken, Steve will be awake, this is the only way to survive and reach safety."

"Is this the only way out of this valley?"

Kevin laughed and replied, "For you two, yes, there is no other way, except as spirits."

Ken laughed and said; "Spirits? Not yet Kevin!"

"When will you report us as missing?" Steve enquired.

"At the end of the day when the cows wander home on their own. I'll have to ask where you are in the valley?"

"What will we find at the other side of the caves?" Ken asked.

Kevin began to give the men an idea of what was in store for themselves in making this escape. He explained that they must not ever leave the water, until the hills were in the far distance, nor undress, as white bodies can be seen clearly in the water. You will sleep in the water, the water will be your home, you will learn to eat fish raw. Your only choice is to stay alive." Kevin added,

"They use specially trained dogs, and the hunt will be full on, you carry vital information and if you leave the water, it's a bad death with the ants."

"How far before the creek enters the river?" Steve asked.

"I'm not sure, but make sure you're in the river before daybreak and keep close to the edge of the bank, well-hidden if you can find old branches in the water. Don't be tempered to take off your boots. You'll have to endure leaches and other nasties, so you will have to use mud on your faces."

"It seems as if the men hunting us will be not the giving up type," Ken mused

"You're correct in that assumption Ken, if you escape, they die a nasty death." Kevin explained.

They left Kevin's hut for the last time and went to milk the cows. This job completed and herding the cows together they began to move them to a richer pasture. To go in the desired direction, they needed to pass through the gate which Kevin was mending.

Kevin spoke quietly looking down at the ground, "Dommy sent a message, they're coming for you both tonight, so goodbye and good luck."

In their own way both men bent down and thanked Kevin, he could only say, "Go now and get into that cave as soon as you can do it safely."

They walked amongst the cows with bent knees as the herd ambled towards fresh water.

It was in the late morning when the cows reached the water, both men crawled in front of the animals and the cows took no notice as they slipped into the water, with the rope tied securely to each other, with enough length for movement. It was a shock going under water with the barest ripple, then rising to the other side in semi-darkness. They saw the split but mercifully the current wasn't too strong and they were able to swim to the left.

In the years ahead, it was a long time before either Ken or Steve could endure to talk about this nightmare journey under the hills in the creek. There were places where they thought they'd die, places where they couldn't hold breath any longer. They endured when the rope was tangled and became the enemy. Ken and Steve came to know each other in ways outside their normal life's experiences, In those caves they were each other's support, if one went so would the other. Once they faced a waterfall and held each other on the edge of the abyss. There was no escape in this place, the only sound of gurgling water, or their voices when an arm or a leg hit a sharp rock. It was not good to draw blood, which drew unwanted attention from things which hurt. They kept swimming and treated each other as close brothers, each had to comfort the other at times in ways that only men who have endured such places or experiences could understand.

How long did it last?

"It felt like forever," Steve said.

Both Ken and Steve felt it was hours of unrelenting water slowly pulling them this way and that as they fought to stay in the main current. The relief in seeing the late afternoon sky was beyond words.

"We can't go out of the cave yet, there will be men watching," Ken commented, adding, "What can you see Steve?"

They didn't remove the rope, remembering Kevin's words, but worked their way close to the undergrowth at the edge of the cave and looked out at the stream. They were shocked to see just about all the undergrowth had been cleared away from the banks. Though there were clumps of dark green reeds growing near the banks.

"I don't trust those reeds, there could be traps in them. Let's take a chance and keep to the left-hand side again and go now," Ken suggested.

They kept as close to the bank as they could, with mud on their faces. The stream was too narrow to hide in daytime, but it was essential to get to the river as quickly as possible. They were strong swimmers so they headed for the river.

CHAPTER 23

James Wade made the ride to Green Hills in record time, knowing what was in the message. He'd made a supreme effort with very little sleep and travelled in the moonlight. Both himself and his horse were obviously exhausted, when he rode into the police barracks yard. Tony Bane had just walked out of the stables and was shocked to see the condition of horse and man and ran to stop James from falling out of his saddle.

"Tony, urgent message for Alex Pitt, is he here?" James said slowly.

"Yes, he arrived early this morning."

"Give it to him please, it's urgent."

After helping James from his horse, Tony took the papers to Alex, while the stable hands assisted James and his horse. He dropped on a pile of straw and was asleep in seconds, the men smiled and left him for several hours.

Alex read the message and handed it to Sergeant Ray Shaw, who after reading it asked, "What men do you want to take out to the river?"

"With the real possibility of trouble, John Hale, Andrew Willow, Ted Swan, Fred Hall, Charley Rush and Bill Todd."

"What about Tony Bane?"

"I'd like him to keep watch on the secret track, because the gossip around the fires at night suggest the 'big man' is coming soon. I want to know when he's entering the valley."

"I've requested thirty Special Constables for the coming major operation, plus any available police, what else do you require?"

"A special group of men to stop anyone leaving the valley through the secret entrance, unless in company with our own police."

"I'll see to it Mr. Pitt"

"Thank you, Sergeant."

"Where is Mr. Wade now?"

Alex smiled briefly, "I'm told asleep in the stable on a pile of straw."

"Exhausted?"

"Totally"

"I know what that feels like, let him be."

"With the message recently delivered by Andrew Willow and now the one by James Wade, our operation is getting closer. We need both Ken Taylor and Steve Baker to fill in the gaps before we can invade the valley," Alex thought out loud.

"Leave Fred Hall to continue doing camp duty out on the tracks, he can give support to Mr. Bane," Sergeant Shaw suggested.

"Yes, that's a good idea, we need all the news we can hear from the valley."

"When do you want to leave here?"

"Tomorrow morning, early if I can get the men and horses moving!"

"What do you need?"

"Two pack horses, with camp ovens, billy cans, quantities of rations, a medical chest. The men can shoot game for the pot."

"Who'll lead this operation to the river?"

"Bill Todd knows where we have to be on the river. At the present he is out on patrol, I'll send John Hale out to find him."

"Is he still searching for the men stealing food from the campers?"

"He's been working the camps not far from here, while picking up useful gossip."

Alex left the Sergeant's office and began preparing for the next morning's official looking patrol. News spread and an excitement was in the air as men began to pack swags and check saddle bags. John Hale rode happily out to find Bill and Andrew Willow left to locate Charley.

"I want him here this afternoon, Andrew, take a spare saddled horse with you." Alex had told him.

*

John found Bill not far from Green Hills. He was talking to a family who had been raided that morning. Bill was given a clear description of the men. He saw John approaching and turned away from the completed discussion. John imparted the news and they rode back to the barracks to find Alex.

"Where did Ian say we had to meet him?" Bill asked him.

"Opposite a dead waterhole."

"That's a very strange place and I'm not likely to forget it," Bill said quietly.

"You do know it, don't you?" Alex asked half afraid.

"I will when I get there!"

"You don't sound in the least sure of it?'

"No, because I try to forget odd places which are second nature to Ian."

"Bill this is a serious patrol; you have to know where you're taking it."

"Don't worry Alex, I'm sure Ian will be there before us."

"There is just one other matter, we're taking Charley as the cook, if we can find him in time?'

"Couldn't have chosen somebody else?" Bill replied wryly.

"No, he's the best cook."

"Perhaps Andrew won't be able to find him. Oh! I do hope so!" Bill grinned and said wishing out loud.

"Bill behave yourself, you know he's the best cook."

"Yes I do, unfortunately.

*

Andrew rode along several tracks in the vicinity of the valley and saw no sign of Charley. He didn't dare stop and ask anyone if they'd seen a shabbily dressed man who liked to walk chewing bones! The mere thought caused Andrew to smile as he rode to the tops of hills and looked everywhere but there was no sign of him. He rode down close to the closed valley, where there were always men moving from place to place, but no sign of him. Andrew was beginning to be concerned; he decided to leave the two horses with the friendly squatter and go on foot. He was much more comfortable in his shabby clothes walking amongst others dressed in a similar fashion. He made good time moving from one camp site to another and all were empty of people. At one site Andrew felt he wasn't alone, he walked ever so quietly and saw a man tied to a tree, creeping up without making a sound, the man was gagged. Andrew recognised him and grinned, before taking his knife and cutting the ropes and at the end reluctantly removing the gag.

"Am I glad to see you Andy, we need to get out of here fast," Charley spoke quietly.

Walking unsteadily at first, Charley gradually lengthened his stride as they kept to the trees.

"Can't talk now, we have to get as far away as we can from here," he said.

There was no way they'd be able to get back to the barracks before nightfall. Charley didn't speak for the first hour, they kept close to the trees, avoiding everyone.

"Andy we can't be seen, where are the horses you told me you had here?" he said later.

"With the friendly squatter."

"Are we close to him?"

"If we walk quickly, probably an hour away."

"Lead on, they'll be looking for me before it gets dark."

Andrew and Charley walked and ran, racing one another, keeping it up until they reached the friendly man who had their horses ready, He was greatly relieved to be on a horse and well away from danger, but he wouldn't talk about what had happened to him.

"Why don't we use that man's name?" Andrew asked.

"It would be sudden death to use his name, because he'd get to hear about it and someone would be dispatched to silence the person," Charley replied.

"That is powerful."

"Yes, in his area of interest and particularly anywhere near this valley."

"I thought the reason might be to give him a name, automatically gave him more power, it's an old way of thinking."

Charley laughed. Andrew was relieved that it was a moonlight night and he knew the road was close to the settlement of Green Hills. By the time he reached the barracks, Charley was swaying in his saddle and didn't look at all well when Andrew last saw him in the twilight, now it was quite dark. There was a light in the stables, a shadow who became a man emerged whom Andrew recognised and asked urgently, "Get Alex Pitt please."

Not only Alex but the Sergeant came promptly down to the stables, giving instructions to the stable hand to look after the horses. Charley and Andrew were escorted to the meal room behind the barracks. After Charley had been supplied with food and a mug of tea, he began to speak.

"Firstly, Steve and Ken have escaped from the valley, no one knows exactly how they've done it, though a suggestion has been made that it was through an underground water course."

This was news which spread like wildfire in the barracks. Charley went on to talk about a group of men at a camp beside the hidden track, which was where he heard about the escape.

"The valley is in uproar about it because Joe is in charge of the lower valley and if the men aren't captured, he'll go to the ants alive. There are groups of men searching for Steve and Ken now," he said.

"How were you caught Charley?" Alex asked.

"I was very close to the camp and heard everything which was said. Unfortunately, one of the men went to take a piss and fell over me."

"What were they going to do with you?" the Sergeant asked.

"They were returning to the valley tonight and taking me to the ants, they thought it might give some amusement to the men. I was overjoyed to see young Andrew come marching down to my tree"

"I was creeping quietly Charley!" Andrew chipped in.

"Didn't matter, though why didn't you instantly take the gag out of my mouth, instead of later?"

The Sergeant hid a sudden desire to laugh, Alex couldn't quite conceal his sudden laughter and Andrew just grinned at Charley.

*

The next morning the patrol left Green Hills and travelled south with enough police and equipment, including pack horses, to cause comments by the other travellers on the tracks. They made good time, with the pack horses inclined to be slower climbing up the hills. With the open plains now in sight, they decided to camp in the last small valley, before riding down to the river.

"Where do you want to set up camp?" Charley asked Alex.

"Beside the creek with a good fishing hole."

"F-fish, don't you ever get sick of eating freshwater fish?"

"Not when there are few other choices, Charley."

"I suppose not."

Between them a place was found and instead of making a fire Charley unloaded the pack horses, sorting out what he'd need for the night. In all the months Charley had spent with the bush police, he had done his best to avoid working with Bill Todd. They always seemed to light each other's fuse, with the least effort. Now Bill rode up to the camp and looking around, said loudly, "What no fire?"

To which Charley, still feeling irritated at being caught, gagged and tied up, replied, "I'm sure you can go without your tea at your age."

Alex gave a look which expressed their thoughts clearly and smiled as Bill replied, "Perhaps you didn't think about it being a city man."

"What's being a man of the f— city got to do with it?" Charley asked, standing up.

"Just making a point Charley."

Not to be the loser in this verbal match, he replied, "If you want a f– drink, go to the creek the same as the horses and dogs do if they're thirsty."

Both Andrew and Alex tried not to laugh at the outraged expression on Bill's face.

With an effort Alex managed to say quietly, "Bill you asked for it, so take it like a man."

"Come on cool down, I'll help you put our part of the camp together." Andrew said to Charley.

Alex managed to keep Bill and Charley apart at either side of the camp, which was difficult with Charley being the cook. When Bill went to get his food, Andrew served him with a smile. Bill didn't return the friendly expression and as he walked away, he heard a soft voice say, "Sour puss!"

For a moment Bill stood still, wanting to lash out at Andrew, but in those few seconds of deciding what action to take, Ted suddenly bumped into him.

"Sorry Bill, I thought you were walking," he said.

Bill growled at Ted, who wondered what he'd done to upset the older constable. Alex, who had been a witness, put a hand under Bill's arm and led him away to a place on the edge of the camp. He didn't say a word. Bill ate his meal in silence, washed his own plate and went to his swag, thinking he was a sour puss, quietly chuckling at Andrew's words. The rest of the camp followed him, it had been a long day. The only sounds came from the tops of the trees as the night life woke up and began to chatter throughout the hours of darkness.

Andrew was first out of his swag in the early morning before sunrise, he made a fire and added a number of quart-pots to the red coals. Neither Bill or Charley spoke to each other with Bill grunting "Thanks" for his plate of meat and damper and Charley replying, equally gruffly, "Don't mention it."

Andrew smiled and both men saw his cheerful expression and knew he was a morning person, like Charley, who commented. Alex, having a fair idea what was coming and knowing full well that Bill was not a morning person or even a mid-morning one intervened.

"Cool it Andrew," he said.

"Yes Mr. Pitt."

"And don't call me Mr. Pitt"

"You're acting like a Mister."

"You're as bad as Charley!"

Andrew laughed and was joined by a couple of the men.

"We don't often have comedy at breakfast and it's good to begin the day with some humour," Ted commented.

Bill had had enough of talking men in the morning and he rolled up his swag, gathered up his belongings into his saddle bag and mounted his horse and waited for the camp to saddle up. He could then lead them down to the river, to his best friend Ian Percy who understood about silence in the mornings.

Chapter 24

The line of police and pack horses crossed the last hill following a track used by other animals through the undergrowth, around clumps of trees, up to the top of the hill. The trees visible on the plain below showed the position of the river. Even the pack horses scented the water and were inclined to keep up a steady pace, by midday they were riding along the banks of the river.

"Does this river have a name?" Alex asked Bill.

"Yes, it's the Macquarie River."

In the mid-afternoon around a long curve of the river, they saw blue smoke and riding closer began to recognise the men as police. Bill cantered up ahead when he saw Ian stand up to greet him. Neither showed the emotion they felt at seeing a friend, other than a handshake lasting a little longer than usual between men. Ian saw Charley and instantly understood, saying, "You'd better stay here with me."

"The others?" Bill asked.

"To another camp further down the river, we are expecting trouble."

Charley was about to dismount when Ian held up his hand and spoke loudly, "Hold it."

Getting their attention he continued, "Your camp is further down the river, we are expecting an attack in the coming days, if Steve and Ken escape to us. Your camp has water on three sides, which might be easier to defend, when we all get together."

"While we're altogether now, everyone is expected to do river patrols, always in pairs. The camps must never be left vacant and anyone near the river is to be noted. Don't be fooled by innocent looking old men. There is death waiting on this river," Alex said.

Ian backed up the words expressed by Alex and added, "Your camp is a couple of miles up from here, we've done a little bit for you. Please see to your defences, this is part of our on-going operation."

"Will we get any extra police?" Alex enquired.

"Yes, Sergeant Green is sending Special Constables and other police to your camp, they will be camping out of sight, but within range if we are attacked. They will join us in our invasion of the valley."

"Do you mind if Bill stays with me?" Ian asked Alex.

Alex tried not to show his relief and replied, "I don't mind at all," but a little quirk of mischief caused him to ask Bill, "Are you sure you want to stay Bill?"

Bill recognised the humour and replied cheerfully, "I'm sure you will be quite capable of running the camp without me Alex."

Bill laughed, knowing all was well between himself and Alex.

Chapter 25

Steve and Ken looked at the depth of the stream and were gratified to see that they could swim down in the current, near the lefthand bank.

"With our clothes being sodden and muddy faces and not causing any ripples, we'll be well hidden Ken." Steve commented.

They swam out of the cave and on the edge of the current moved steadily down the creek. It was good to get out of the dark cave and into natural light, except both places were dangerous. They were tired from the swim in the caves, being young and fit in the stream, they had to swim for life. The stream was fast moving and narrow with nowhere to hide for any length of time, Both were strong swimmers, and it was well into twilight when at last they entered the river. Steve saw a clump of half-submerged logs on their side and suggested, "Ken, we're exhausted and we need to sleep, I'll take the first watch and you sleep."

Using the rope which kept Ken's head out of the water, gradually a method was developed which served the men, as long as they were in the water, to sleep in reasonable comfort for the conditions in which they had to endure, never leaving the water.

On the first morning Ken suggested, "We're going to need an organized plan to survive the water. It will be dangerous to swim in the daylight hours all the time, yet we have to get as far away from the hills as possible."

"We have to eat and all of it will be uncooked meat," Steve said with a groan.

Ken smiled, before saying, "We'll manage Steve, there are all kinds of life forms in the water which we can eat and eat well."

Steve's expression made Ken want to laugh and ducked his head under the water to cool it and the bubble of amusement.

"I assume you have your knives?" Ken asked, shaking the water from his face.

"Yes, they never leave me."

"Good for catching fish Steve, forget about what the water will do to the blades, we will have days in this water."

In the distance they heard dogs barking and Ken spoke with a sigh, "The hunt has begun Steve, we'll continue to swim every day and sleep when we can find shelter in the water."

The search was relentless, day after day men with dogs combed the riverbanks, they set fire to reeds and the built-up of sticks and logs, left by floods in the river. Mercifully the fires were always behind them as they desperately kept ahead of the hunters though their hours of sleep became shorter. One good aspect of the fires was that half-burnt animals fell into the water trying to escape, providing them with much needed food.

They were incredibly careful not to be seen by dogs or men with their hair, beards and faces muddied. Only the whites of their eyes revealed the culture which were shaded by grass and leaves.

"I think the dogs scent us or are aware of us, but as long as they never see us, we will be safe." Ken told Steve in a whisper.

Exhaustion wasn't an option, as each one slept the other stayed awake, giving as much time as possible to rest and sometimes more than the allotted time. Steve woke up to this fact and told Ken, "You need it more than I do, and you must rest properly."

"We are still wearing our clothes and boots, these wear us down and make swimming hard, I can hardly wait to discard them."

"I know they do weigh us down and like you I want to be rid of them, but not just yet."

Ken recognised both himself and Steve were getting weaker, yet were so strong in the mind that neither would give up the fight to win their freedom. During the moonlight nights, Ken saw the shadows of men searching for any sign of them. Food became hard to find, and this affected their strength, they'd die in the water before giving up.

One morning they heard horses, quite a lot of horses and men in police uniforms. Steve wanted to call out, but Ken put his hand over his mouth.

"It could be a trap, we'll go on for a while and see if the hunters are still following us," he whispered.

They continued swimming for another two days, until they couldn't hear any dogs or men.

"It's quiet here," Steve commented.

They kept undercover on the right-hand side of the bank, when suddenly they saw a dark skinner man dive into their deep pool, his head came up and they recognised Ian Percy. Their relief was beyond words and stayed quietly to see who would be joining him. Sure enough, Bill Todd dived into the pool, but he went into the pool with his eyes open and in that instant, saw four white eyes watching him. In total shock he called out to Ian, in a voice filled with emotion, "They're here, Steve and Ken are here."

Bill swam across to them and not saying another word, put out a hand to touch each man. There were sudden tears in his eyes, or it could have been water dripping from his hair, and said in a choked voice, "You made It."

Their clothes were in disarray, only just staying together, their state was very poor. Ian called out for help and Alex who had come up to their camp to talk, unhesitatingly entered the water to assist. Oddly enough they didn't want to be separated and clung to each other as they were removed from the water. Those who saw them for the first time out of the water were deeply shocked at their condition, they'd obviously starved and were gaunt looking. They had survived an unimaginable number of days in the water, fully clothed to hide their white skin and had used enormous strength to keep ahead of fire and dogs. It was a swim with the odds of death or life.

"I can take Steve and Ken to our camp, if you approve, they need good care and careful feeding, Charley understands what this entails," Alex suggested.

"How will you move them, neither Ken nor Steve are able to walk at the present time," Bill asked.

"I can use the sledge which we brought the supplies up to you on." He suddenly smiled and said, "Charley and Andrew put it together and told me they thought it could be useful in a day or so!"

Bill walked across the camp to examine it and was surprised to see a couple of wounded men could ride on it with care, it had a few animal skins on it already.

He turned to Alex asking, "How did Charley know how to make it?"

"When he left school."

Seeing Bill's expression Alex said, "He did go to school for a short period, up to sixth class, I believe. Later he worked at the hospital making these kinds of useful things to move men and women carefully."

Steve and Ken were moved on to the sledge and gently pulled down to the other camp. Charley was waiting for them with a little quantity of food and two swags close together. The men were barely conscious, ate the food and were asleep in no time.

Chapter 26

The new police who had recently been appointed to Hill Top had accompanied Roy to the second camp. Alf Stokes and Willie Darkwood built an enclosure on the top side of the camp, with an added space as requested by Charley.

"A night nurse to keep an eye on them," he'd said.

He had insisted that both Steve and Ken only eat a small amount of food, this was mainly liquid with tiny pieces of meat in it.

"Anymore and they'll be sick, their stomachs have shrunk in size, it'll take a day or two to get each man back to normal."

After their simple meal both men, totally exhausted, fell into a deep sleep. While they slept Charley and Andrew removed their sodden clothes and boots, revealing a multitude of scratches, bites and other cuts on their skin, which required instant attention with what little medical equipment had been sent by Sergeant Green. For a brief time Bill and Charley were of the same mind, as Bill had a knowledge of bush remedies.

By the time Bill finished administering, Charley looked down at Steve and Ken and said, "They're got more leaves on them than a F– tree!"

"Many of those bites will be gone by morning and it will stop that rash from spreading,"

"Where did you learn this stuff?" Charley asked.

"Staying alive in the bush and listening to those who knew what was safe to use for various ailments."

Charley recognised Bill's effort to be helpful and took it at face value.

"Thanks for your help, we don't have a lot of choices out here and anything which is a help to Ken and Steve, is okay with me," he said.

Bill tried to find the words to reply to Charley who had been quite gracious to him, and couldn't locate any in the same style, so just said, "Just get them well so we can ask questions."

Charley understood and grinned at him and said, "Give them a day or so and then ask simple questions, but don't you F— tire them out, remember Steve and Ken are sick men."

Charley watched Bill turn on his heel and walk away, knowing he'd be feeling irritated because he'd lost the upper hand, Charley smiled and turned to the men, making sure they were still asleep. Bill walked away thinking that Charley was an old bastard in any language, and he was amazed that he'd worked in a hospital. Another smile and Bill thought, I must tell Ian if ever I get sick, don't put me into the care of Charley!

The first night Roy stood watch with Andrew and talked quietly. After about three hours, Ken was the first to cry out, "Steve, I can't feel Steve, if I let him drown he'll die and I'll have let my friend down, Steve where are you?"

Roy woke Ken and said, "Ken you're safe, see Steve's head is above water."

Ken's eyes glazed over and for a few minutes he held on to Roy, before sleep took him away again. Later Steve had to be assured Ken's head was above water. During the hours of the night Ken and Steve constantly awoke to check on the other, with never any more than a few hours of constant sleep, before a fear of letting the other down. Perhaps the worst fear was being on their own in a hostile environment and being hunted. Roy and Andrew experienced one night of what they had endured for a number of days. It was a relief when the sun rose in the eastern sky and Roy and Andrew could go to their swags.

When Steve and Ken awoke and saw each other covered in reeds, leaves and even some bark and something else they couldn't identify, they smiled at each other.

Charley gave them some food explaining in a kind voice, "You've been without proper food for days and we have to build your stomachs up again slowly, a lot of food now wouldn't be good for you."

Andrew who had been listening, said in surprise, "You didn't swear at them Charley!"

"No, you can't F___ swear at sick people."

Andrew wasn't the only one who smiled at hearing these words from the make-shift sick bay!

Keeping Steve and Ken resting was nigh on impossible, the nights were bad and they had to be woken on a regular basis, in the daytime they walked, stumbled, fell over, got up and tried again, holding on to each other. It took a couple of days to master the art of walking, all the time eating a bit more food, and Charley couldn't be bribed to give them anymore! They did try and he wasn't above whacking a hand who attempted to seize another slice of meat, saying, "When I say no, I mean it, tomorrow we'll see."

"Why not now?" Steve asked.

"I don't know who gave you that extra food this morning, but I did see you both being sick behind the logs up the creek a bit."

On the third day they insisted on dressing in their uniforms, which now were far too big for their slight frames, the holes in their leather belts moving up several spaces. Each night they slept on swags close together and the nightmares continued.

"Do you mind seeing Ken so close to Steve?" Alex asked Roy.

"Not in the least Alex, they need each other's support after their shared hell together. It will be many months before they can live apart from one another."

Alex let the matter go, though he did wonder if the many months would be longer than expected by Roy. While Steve and Ken were improving themselves, they had to be available to answer questions about the valley. At the present time they were giving details to the Government Agent concerning the location of the counterfeiting operation.

Slowly everything they'd seen in the hidden valley was revealed to Alex, Bill, Ian and the other police in the camp. Notes were taken and detailed messages sent on a regular basis to Sergeant Green. In this way smaller uniforms arrived for Steve and Ken, the others were kept until the time when their weight improved.

Ken and Steve also noted the names of those men who saved their lives or helped them in any way, in particular Kevin and Dommy. A Senior Officer who had come to question the men made it plain that he had no interest in saving anyone from the valley.

"They are criminals and will go to a road gang, bad men I will see them hang," he said.

"No Sir, we gave them our word," Ken said firmly.

The Senior Officer wasn't accustomed to having the word 'no' said to him by a junior policeman.

"I will see at the time, the matter is now closed," he replied.

"No Sir, we want your word now," Steve said firmly

"You are under orders"

"Without Kevin and Dommy, we would be dead now, we gave our word as policemen to these men, so as far as we're concerned, that's final," Ken replied.

The Senior Officer stared at the two men who dared to question his authority and decided not to take offence this time.

"Alright, I'll give you my word they will be free men, if you get them out of the valley before my troops arrive in that hell hole. Do you understand." he said firmly.

"Yes Sir," both men said together, adding, "We will Sir, thank you."

Steve and Ken walked away to the other side of the camp and didn't hear the Senior Officer say to Alex, "Mr. Pitt, those are two brave men but later tell them it isn't wise to say no to a man of my rank."

Alex tried not to smile and this was observed by the Senior Officer, who commented, "Are you thinking they might not take any notice of my reprimand?"

Alex could only say very carefully, "Sir, they're bush police, and their word is more valuable than your reprimand, while you reside in a faraway city."

A silence.

"You were in my command area."

"Yes Sir."

"I think you must now be serving in bad company."

"Just different Sir," Alex grinned.

"It must be."

"How is Charley Rush coping with the bush police?"

"You know Charley Sir!" Alex laughed.

"I'm glad at least one of you is normal!"

He turned his horse and rode away with his escort of six troopers towards the distant hills.

For the rest of the day Ken and Steve now had a purpose to build themselves up, the saving of their friends, and sheer bloody determination played a major part in their plan.

"You don't have to do everything the hard way," Charley said to Steve.

"Yes, we do Charley, we have to get a lot better to be able to go to the valley to rescue Kevin, Dommy and a couple of others, before that F__ Senior Officer goes into it."

Charley was surprised and spoke to Andrew, "Did you hear what Steve just said to me?"

"I would've been deaf not to have heard it, Charley!"

"We'll help them get fit. I agree those men who helped them ought to be saved. I know that F__ Senior Officer, if he catches them first, they'll go to a road gang for sure."

By the fourth morning Ken and Steve were firmly on the way to a full recovery and left the covered area to join the men in the main camp.

Chapter 27

While Steve and Ken had been kept in isolation, the rest of the camp had duties to perform patrolling the countryside and keeping watch on any unusual activities. Ian and Bill had requested Alex to send the two new policemen who had recently been appointed to Hill Top, Willie Darkwood and Alfred Stokes to patrol the river with them.

Ian had explained to the new men what this work entailed, emphasising, "You must not be seen or even give these men an idea that they are being watched."

"You know what they are doing and it's vital we know too," Bill added.

Willie, whose eyesight was excellent at long distances, watched the men slowly combing the riverbanks on the left-hand side. Clumps of reeds were being set on fire along with any driftwood close to the water.

"Have they seen us, Willie?" Ian asked.

"No Ian." He stopped talking and said slowly, almost in disbelief, "They have a man in the water too, though he is walking and hanging on to a stick being held by another man on the bank."

Progress was slow and determined which was quite obvious to Bill.

"Perhaps it's time we moved down to the main camp," he suggested to Ian.

"I agree, I just don't like leaving a good swimming pool."

While they were talking about moving camp, Willie and Alf were watching the men on the riverbank.

"How long do you think they will take to reach Bill's camp and know Ken and Steve are out of the water?" Willie asked.

Bill and Ian stopped talking to hear Alf's reply.

"That's not the point Willie, it's a small group of men now, I'd want to know if a horseman leaves that group."

"What am I missing Alf?"

He patted Willie on the shoulder and laughed before saying "It's what I'd do if I was the leader of that lot of men."

Bill and Ian sat perfectly still on their horses as they digested those words.

"You've been in the army?" Ian spoke to Alf.

"Yes, and someone needs to watch the hills behind that group of men carefully."

Ian thought carefully and suggested, "I'll tell Alex what you've said Alf, he's in charge of this Operation. I think you and Willie should patrol the river and gather whatever news of their intentions is possible to pass on to Alex, Bill or myself. Just don't get caught because we won't be able to rescue you. We won't bargain with criminals; it never works out to our advantage."

On the evening of the fourth day Willie and Alf approached Alex in early twilight, as he was sitting talking to Bill and Ian.

Alex asked them to sit down at the fire, asking Alf, "What news do you bring to us?"

"We've been keeping watch on the men up the river. Two days ago they made a camp and sent a man back for re-enforcements."

"How do you know?"

Willie smiled and answered quietly, "I can swim Alex and went up the river last night and listened to their conversation, they know Ken and Steve are out of the water."

Alex asked in a dangerous tone of voice, "Why am I only hearing about it now Willie?'

"There was a cave in the bank above where I was hiding, only when the camp was asleep could I escape, I arrived back here a couple of hours ago, so you are hearing about it now.'

Alex wasn't entirely satisfied, "So that's why we couldn't find you."

"Yes Alex, our job is to watch the river."

"What about you Alfred?"

"Keeping a watch out for Willie and getting worried when he didn't return in the usual time."

"Do you mean that Willie has done this work before this event?"

"Yes of course, how do you think we get information Alex?"

Bill and Ian tried to dampen the rising anger in Alex by saying, "Alf has had army experience and knows what he's doing, he knows you're in charge and he has something to say, so please listen."

Alf spoke quietly and firmly, "We can't defend this camp on the bend of the river."

"Why can't we defend it?" Alex asked, still feeling irritated.

"Alf tell him," Willie said.

"Men coming out of the water with knives, while you're shooting at men in front of you. I don't like your chances of surviving an onslaught of determined men."

Alex turned to Bill and Ian and said, "Well don't just stand there, what do you think Ian?"

"Alf, how long do we have to make up our minds?" Ian asked.

"This is the crux of the matter; I'd say by tomorrow it'd be too late."

"Didn't Sergeant Green send Special constables out here?" Bill asked.

"Yes, he did and they are camped out of sight of the river at the present time," Alex replied.

"Who's in charge of those men?"

"George Nash, a Hill Top policeman."

Alex sighed, turned again to face Alf and said, "I've heard you've had army experience, even though now you're a junior police officer, how would you defend this camp?'

"I wouldn't try and defend it, I'd set fires and make-believe swags, a camp sleeping. Take the horses up the river out of the way, everyone else on the other side of the bend of the river, with guns firing while other men are loading them into a camp of invading men."

Alex relaxed, now he saw a way ahead and said with a grin, "We'll do it. Steve and Ken will be behind us and the Special constables in front hiding amongst the trees."

Alex had the grace to say to Alf and Willie, "Never mind me I get grumpy sometimes, thank you for your getting the information, I don't want to think what would have happened without it."

"When would you expect the attack?" Bill asked Willie.

"After dawn tomorrow morning."

"How would you move the basic camp across the river, without the men knowing what we were doing here?" Ian asked Alf.

"Willie and I found a crossing a couple of miles below here, the old gum trees are thick on the other side of the river, we thought the thirty Special constables could cross at that place. There is enough room for them to hobble their horses and walk up to positions overlooking this camp."

"Steve and Ken?" Ian enquired.

"Could be behind the undergrowth at the back of the constables, with Charley and Andrew, armed naturally."

"Where will the rest of us be?"

"Beside the Special constables."

"Does your mind give you a picture of what this camp ought to be like at dawn," Ian said.

"You take your swags and anything you value to a new camp on the other side of the river. In this camp it will show men sleeping with smouldering fires and the scent of meat cooking for the men riding out at dawn."

"Do we leave traps?"

Alf laughed and replied cheerfully, "Yes, anything to make them think twice about a second visitation to us!"

"I'll quietly organise our withdrawal to the new position. I'll leave you, Alf and Willie, to plan some surprises, ask Ted if he has any ideas."

"I'll ride out to the Special constables camp and get them moving," Ian volunteered.

Each of the men went to inform all those concerned in this plan, and regardless of how serious the attack could be, there was a feeling of excitement in the camp.

It was a busy night, with hardly a sound as the men worked in creating a camp which wasn't a real one, enjoying the experience of digging holes and covering them. Ted thought of putting sharp sticks in the bottom of the holes on the edge of the camp. Mercifully it was a moonlight night, and the other camp was set up without any fires. By dawn every man was in his place and waiting. Alf pointed at the shadows of men walking quietly just out of the tree line. Willie indicated with his hand several men swimming down the river.

"This is a well-planned attack," Alf whispered to Bill.

Even in the bad light Steve recognised Joe out in front of a group of men and whispered to Charley, "He will fight to the very end to capture Ken and me, if he can't get us he will die here, this will be a better death than what is waiting for him back in the valley."

*

The invading men came quietly into the camp, until some slipped into the holes and there were shouts of fury, then the bullets were fired into the sleeping forms. Joe was the first to realise the camp was empty of bodies and at that moment the full force of the police fired at the invaders. There were no logs to retreat to in the vicinity of the camp, these had been removed out of harm's way. Having no place to hide behind, it was slaughter, Steve saw Joe go down and remain still, where others tried crawling towards trees away from death. Surprisingly enough, apart from the whine of the bullets, it was remarkably quiet close to the ground. On the tree tops the birds were full of chatter as a couple of hawks smelt blood and came to investigate.

Charley and Andrew were kept busy attending to wounded police, no one was killed on their side of the river. The attack failed and as the sun rose above the distant hills, Special constables were rounding up those who attacked the camp and arrested them with several needing medical attention of one kind or another. Those who were unharmed were made to dig some graves on a small rise of land.

Ken and Steve were relieved to be far enough away not to hear the sobs, crying with the fear of what now lay before those captured. Ian had seen two men escape by going into the water, he noticed one man had been bleeding quite badly. He'd drawn another policeman's attention to them, and a couple of shots were fired in their direction which missed their targets.

"He probably hit a fish or two!" Bill, who was near him, said.

Steve and Ken had taken part at the beginning of the fight, but had to withdraw, due to a lack of energy. For the few minutes they found it satisfying, though a telling one that they were simply not ready to hold their own in a serious action. They had retreated back to the camp and talked quietly, drinking cold tea.

"I've never been so weak, and I don't like it," Ken expressed.

"Same here. We'll just have to keep improving ourselves, we'll never give up and I think we'll do our exercises in private," Steve agreed.

"Steve, we'll need to take a couple of the police with us into the valley to rescue Kevin, Dommy and a couple of other men, also a pack horse for Kevin's belongings." Ken suggested.

"I think in the initial attack and just afterwards it will be a dangerous place. Kevin's hut is isolated and ought to be reasonably safe, though the milking shed is close," Steve agreed adding.

Ken seemed to be labouring with a thought and at last brought it to the surface, as Steve watched him with a smile.

"I'd like to request Alex for mounted policemen whom we know will be guided by our knowledge once we are in the valley. Our concern is for those who saved us, we'll have to get them out before the other police see what has been happening on the northern end."

Steve again agreed and spoke in a soft tone of voice, "We don't know for sure, but if it's true, none of our friends will be safe. There will be a natural fury."

"How much can we tell Alex?"

"I think they're aware we haven't told them everything about the valley. I'm not prepared to tell him anything. Though we need to impress upon him the need to get in and out quickly without delays of any kind," Steve responded carefully.

"Where are we going after leaving the valley with the men?"

"I've learnt there's a Squatter friendly to police in the hill not far from the valley and we'll need Andrew with us." Steve replied.

"We can't leave them close to the valley."

"What about later taking them down to the ranges?"

"Do you mean to Red Bryant's place.?"

"It's the best solution to a tricky problem."

Chapter 28

In the middle of the morning after the attack, Alex received a message to say the man and his escort had entered the valley.

"The entrance to the closed valley is now sealed by a group of police," he was delighted to announce to his colleagues.

George Nash had come to speak to Alex and listened to this news.

"Most of my men are unhurt and ready to ride, but I'll be leaving four men with Charley. There is nothing seriously wrong with them, except for a couple of bullets which need to be removed," he said.

"I'd like you to take Steve and Ken with you plus Roy, Andrew, Alf and Willie," Alex asked.

He explained their desire to rescue four men out of the valley, at the time when the police entered it.

"A tricky situation, they will definitely need to be at the entrance as soon as the police move in. I intend to travel at a fast rate, The men travelling with Steve and Ken will need to double up if those men get tired," George understood instantly and replied.

"That's been explained to them. We're also leaving this morning and going straight to the valley," Alex said.

"That's where we are heading, I received a message telling me that more police are on their way there plus Government Agents.'

"They're not taking any chances of him escaping, are they?" Alex mused. "He's a slippery bastard; anything is possible and there've been whispers about something on the northern end of the valley which is deadly."

"Recently?" Alex asked.

"Over a period of months. Alex, we'll meet at the valley, I must get going now."

Alex went to find Steve before he left the camp and asked, "Did you tell us everything you saw in the closed valley?"

"We told you everything we actually saw during our time there."

"What about what you didn't see and heard about?"

Ken, who was nearby, said, "Alex, the valley wasn't the kind of community where asking questions was safe. We reported on what we saw in the lower valley."

"I think you are avoiding the question, and I'm not convinced those four men ought to be removed until we know more about the situation in the valley."

"Alex it isn't your place to judge what we endured in the valley," Steve said quietly.

George had come up with his horse and said to Steve and Ken, "I'm ready to ride now."

He turned to Alex and suggested, "You can sort out this problem at the Squatter's farm later."

Alex handed over a piece of paper, almost reluctantly, giving permission for the four men to be allowed to leave the closed valley in the company of the six police.

Steve and Ken thanked him and mounted their horses and left the camp.

*

The half day's ride was enough for Steve and Ken but neither liked admitting that they lacked the stamina to ride all day. When questioned they were inclined to say they'd be better the next day, which didn't deceive George for one moment

"Your horse is strong, you take Steve and Andrew can take Ken, Roy and Willie can lead your horses," he smiled and said to Alf.

It was a relief when George called a halt in twilight and within a short period of time campfires were burning as the light faded. No one noticed when Steve and Ken took Roy out seemingly to check on the horses. Steve explained about the rescue of the four men and why the six of them were involved in this job. Ken talked a bit more about the valley.

"They were not involved in our time in what was happening at the upper end of the valley," he said.

"Roy, we want you to take them in the direction of the Squatter and once out of sight of everyone connected to the valley, turn south and travel as far as you can before camping. If you can get the two men who worked with the cows into a droving camp a long way from here, this would be a good solution. As for Kevin and Dommy, we want them taken down to Red Bryant's place. Kevin has his own packhorse which we supplied for him," Steve continued.

Roy grinned and laughed and after he retrieved his breath said, "Someone is not going to be pleased with you when they discover these men are not where they're meant to be!!"

"Don't you worry about us; our concern is getting these men to safety."

"Are you sure you'll be alright, I did hear that a Senior Officer had been rough with you and Ken," Roy asked.

"We aren't worried, so you don't need to worry, Roy."

They returned to the campfires and joined the conversations and the laughter.

*

The next morning the men were on their horses before sunrise. Steve and Ken were unaware they were being watched, as they desperately kept sitting slightly forward on their saddles, showing a determination not to wilt in the early Autumn sunlight. Even so, it takes a fit man to stay in a saddle all day. Ken and Steve kept riding and refused to give in to the pain, until George called a halt. They were put on another's horse for the remainder of the day. That night George came and sat beside Ken and Steve and began to talk quietly.

"I've been hearing a lot about what has been going on in that closed valley for a couple of years. To rescue those four men, it will have to be as soon as the police enter, before they get to see things, because after that no one will escape the anger of the police."

Steve and Ken nodded.

"I hope you've made a good plan, because I think a large number of men will hang and the rest will go to chain gangs of various types," George continued.

Ken spoke equally softly, "We understand George, we lived there for some months."

"You and Steve can see good people in the valley, but no one else will see it the way you do, once they know everything about it. Even if you get your men out the law will want them too, make no mistake about it," George said, interrupting him.

"George, we do understand there will be hell to pay, we'll help four men who were good to us, who helped us escape," Steve spoke firmly.

"I know Steve, but the law is often blind to a simple truth. It likes its share of blood too."

On the last day, both Ken and Steve stayed on their saddles all day, refusing to give in to their own pain and secretly won the admiration of their colleagues, even if they needed help to dismount at a camp outside the closed valley.

Alex arrived in the early evening and another group of police arrived from a settlement called Spring Ridge east of Green Hills, within half a day's ride away.

The next morning George led his Troops down onto the secret track leading into a dry creek bed and followed it into a large cave about forty feet high and almost eighty yards wide, the dry creek bed had been made into a road. Behind this group of men was Steve, who was remembering his entry into this valley blindfolded and the sudden cold. The archway was just as impressive and, like the other end, they faced a wall of undergrowth to hide it. One of George's men soon discovered how to move it aside and remounting rode into the valley. A cry went up indicating they'd been seen by the lookout man who instantly rang a bell.

Steve led his group down the side of the valley amongst the trees to the milking sheds.

He saw Kevin and greeted him, followed by Ken who said, "You are looking well Kevin."

"All the better for seeing you two."

"Kevin, we have a packhorse for you, but we don't have much time. Andrew and Roy will help you pack up what you can take with you, but you do have to hurry. Where are the two cowmen?"

"They have their packs here and swags, they are opening the gates for the cows to roam over the valley."

Where's Dommy?" Ken asked.

"He's coming, his gear is here too. He brought it here over a few days when we heard that the man had come, so we knew you wouldn't be too far behind him."

The two cowmen walked up and greeted Steve and Ken cheerfully, it was quite obvious that these were all friends.

Willie began to feel nervous and said, "We have to get out of here. Can you two cowmen ride horses?"

"Yes, we can ride."

"Well tie up your bundles and swags and mount up."

"Are you ready to move now?" Willie called out to Roy.

"In a moment Willie, don't panic just yet!"

"He's here!" Kevin said loudly.

Dommy hurried to Kevin's hut and found his bundle before greeting Steve and Ken.

"We heard you had escaped and there was hell to pay, Joe sent one unfortunate man to the ants and he took a long time to die. It was pitiful, though it was a relief when he went silent," he said.

Dommy's words were a total shock to Roy, Andrew, Willie and Alf.

Ken explained carefully, "Everyone was forced to watch executions of this nature, unfortunately for Dommy he's the cook at the quarters reserved for the men who run the valley, the pit isn't far from his hut."

"How did you endure it?" Andrew asked.

Dommy was a short man, a bit on the slim side for a cook and at this moment couldn't think of a reply, it wasn't a question which could be answered in this valley.

In the silence Ken said, "Andrew, it wasn't about endurance, it was about survival. It was so easy to be put in the pit, if the leader felt you were against him."

"Can you ride a horse?" Steve asked Dommy.

"Yes, I can."

"Well get up on this one and let's get out of here."

They entered the cave after showing the paper of permission, and the relief at riding out into the sunshine of a free environment, caused Dommy to wipe a tear from his eye.

"I was captured the same as Ken and Steve. In the valley it was better not to think, just keep your head down and work. Ken and Steve changed that idea and we were able to help them escape. Now Kevin and I are free with our two friends, the cowmen."

There were still groups of police waiting to enter the cave, as they rode past them at the entrance to the valley. Steve and Ken thanked their friends for their assistance.

"We will join you later in the morning, we'll set up our camp at Kevin's hut," Steve said.

Steve, Ken and Roy rode with Keven, Dommy and the cowmen, in the direction of the friendly Squatter, knowing they were being observed until they were out of sight. All this time Steve and Ken explained the plan for their escape, and they understood the need to get as far away as possible before nightfall.

There were firm handshakes and Steve watched them depart as Ken asked, "Where did you find the horses?"

"In the horse yard of the Special constables, they aren't police horses and can't be traced."

Ken laughed and lent over and patted him on the shoulder, asking, "The packhorse too?"

"Yes."

They both laughed and rode back down into the cave and along the valley floor to Kevin's hut and were pleased to find their old bunks in place, though at the present time covered in other stuff.

"Steve, when we leave here, we'll take anything Kelvin had to leave behind in his rush to escape," Ken commented.

"Do the search now Ken, he kept some papers buried below his bunk, if you find them put them in your saddle bag. I think before they leave here, they will burn all the dwellings, so we need to be ready to go at a moment's notice."

*

In the late afternoon the lower valley was firmly held by the police and the counterfeiting buildings had been burnt down, after the equipment had been dismantled and taken away in drays. There'd been some shooting and this resulted in two graves being dug. The remainder of the men had been captured and chained, then taken out of the valley, followed by the men taken at the camp near the secret entrance.

Andrew, Willie and Alf had been involved in this action and had seen the pit of meat ants, which were still eating a human body and were still reeling from the shock.

"I thought there'd be more bones," Andrew said.

"Look down the hill behind the pit," Ken replied.

"Where is the cemetery?" Willie asked.

Ken refrained from showing any emotion and replied, "There isn't one, no one is buried here, the pit takes care of this problem, alive or dead."

There was silence.

Alex, who had arrived with Bill and Ian, was in time to hear this short conversation, asked, "Does it get any worse from what we've seen today?'

Ken looked at Steve and remained silent.

Alex again spoke, "Does your silence mean yes?"

"Alex you will only ever see the shadow of what has gone on for years in this valley. Your job is to bring it to an end," Steve answered.

As they were talking Andrew approached Ian and said, "Ian, there's a messenger here from Sergeant Green, who wants to speak to you."

Ian walked over to where the man was standing, who asked, "Mr. Percy, I've been searching for you for several weeks, I hope it isn't anything important."

Ian looked at it and replied, "No. Thank you."

As the messenger left the camp, Ian read, *'Mrs. Green goes to church and she didn't think that particular Sunday would suit me. Nice try Mr. Percy!'*

"Anything interesting," Bill asked.

"No Bill."

Later he explained it to Bill who laughed, an unusual emotion in this place of sorrows.

Later in the evening three men came in ordinary clothes to talk to Steve. Alex demanded to know who they represented, so papers were produced and accepted. Steve walked away from the campfire, taking the three men with him, and after a few minutes he called out, "Alf, come here please."

Alf came promptly and in the early twilight recognised one of the men, who before Alf could speak said, "No name, please Alf."

Alf grasped his hand and then hugged him saying, "I know why you're here and it's a good place for you to be, how can I help you?"

"You know each other?" Steve said in surprise.

"We were children together and Alf was fond of my little sister Julie. He was also a friend of my other brother, Frank," the man replied

"Then my three friends disappeared out of the life on the street and now I meet you again after all those years. How is Julie?"

"I'll tell you later, Alf."

Alf noticed blood on his friend's sleeve and asked, "Are you okay, not hurt?"

"A Senior Officer gave orders for a beast to be killed for meat to be distributed to the troops for tomorrow, we did the killing and now the trained butchers have taken over the work of cutting it up," he laughed and replied.

"Will you go with these men tomorrow; they'll explain their needs to you?" Steve asked Alf.

"I'll be delighted to assist an old friend."

"Thanks Alf, we'll see you tomorrow."

Alf and Steve returned to the campfire and Alf said softly, "You know Steve, Alex will always suspect that you know more than you ever tell him."

"Alex is a fine policeman, who has never learnt to get his hands dirty in getting justice."

"And you have?"

"I've lived in this valley with Ken and we've seen more than we ever want to know or remember."

The next day Steve and Ken remained at the hut, as all their friends joined the other police in attacking the northern enclosure. At midday Andrew and Willie returned to the hut with white faces and asked Ken, "Have you been up there?"

"Yes, we've both been commanded to carry buckets of milk, when the normal carriers were sick," Ken answered.

"You saw the mines with holes only tiny enough for little children?" Andrew asked in deep shock, before continuing, "We were told they'd only get food if they handed over gold, the quantity of gold was equal to the food they were given. If they got sick, or hurt or too big to work, they were sent alive to the pit of ants,"

"Behind the pit down at the back of it, there were lots and lots of bones and small skulls. One of the women said that they became accustomed to the cries in the pit, a bit like a dog barking, and after a while they didn't hear the cries of the children in the pit," Willie spoke almost in a whisper.

"We can hardly wait to get out of here," Andrew said.

Willie agreed with him and said, "You could have warned us."

"Would you have believed us if we'd told you?"

"No. We wouldn't have believed that such an awful event could happen in this modern world," Willie replied sadly.

"That is why we remained silent. You had to see it to believe it."

They were unable to comfort their colleagues, except to provide hot mugs of tea and leave them on their own to come to terms with such horrendous crimes.

Chapter 29

Meanwhile, Alf and his three men crossed the valley floor and listened to the story of his friend.

"We were taken from the street by the catchers and brought here. You might remember that my younger sister Julie could be a bit sooky. The man used her as an example, he stripped her and dropped her into the pit of ants, my other brother kicked him hard, he was also stripped and joined Julie. We were forced to watch and listen for several hours. I eventually escaped, but now I'm back again."

Alf noticed one of the men was carrying a billy can with a lid and wondered what was in it.

"What do you want me to do?" he asked.

"Take us to where the man is and leave us."

"Done. I'll make sure no one interrupts whatever it is you have to do."

"He has too many powerful friends to be convicted or ever see inside a court room," his friend explained.

*

The men had no problem entering the complex of structures, with police arresting the women who had been responsible for the children. The police were shocked at what they had uncovered, half-starved children, often sick and in a cage near the pit. They could also hear the little children in the mines in tiny low tunnels, too afraid to come out into the light.

Alf remained calm as they searched for the one man they wanted to address, but at last they found a Senior Officer who bailed the four men up.

"I have an important man here, who came in with the police and now needs an escort to the other side of the cave entrance. Will you take him, I have to go elsewhere?" he said.

"Yes Sir, we'd be pleased to assist you," Alf stated in a fine tone of voice.

"Thank you, I'll see him later this afternoon," the Senior Officer said.

They found the old man sitting in a small room reading a newspaper and he was recognised instantly. He looked up and greeted the men cheerfully.

"Come with us, Sir," one of the men said.

The men left the area of activities and skirted around the entrance to the mine, where police were trying to extract the tiny children.

"It's a waste of time, they'll be dead soon by the look of them," the old man said.

The track started going down the hill past the children's pit. When they neared it the man with the can removed the lid and sprinkled blood on the old man.

"That's clever, some police will think I've been wounded," he said, adding, "Not that much, I'm drenched in cows' blood," then "Stop it, you idiots, I'll have you whipped."

"I don't think so, not today," one of the men said.

"You can't see them yet, but there are dozens of white hands reaching out to you to come to them today," Alf's friend said as the man stood on the edge of the children's pit.

There was an instant moment of knowledge and a cry of terror, "NOoooo…"

As he fell down into the place he had designed for so many, he may not have seen the tiny white hands, but he felt the many mouths seeking the blood.

Alf and the men continued to walk down the track, at the bottom Alf shook hands with the men as they proceeded to the entrance and away back to a distant city.

Alf returned to Kevin's hut and later said to Steve, "He fell into the children's pit."

"A fitting end, Alf."

"What will happen now that he has gone?"

"Those in power will look for him, perhaps even see his remains in the pit."

"He was an evil man."

"We knew that since we were children, Alf."

Alex arrived in the late afternoon and asked Steve, "Where is Roy?"

"I've no idea, Alex."

"I sent men to arrest those four men on the directions of the Senior Officer. The Squatter didn't know anything about them, so where are they Steve?"

"I said I don't know Alex."

"'You didn't send them to that place?"

"No."

"Where did you send them?"

"Alex, we gave our word, and so did that Senior Officer."

"That was before he saw the children in the mines."

"His word is his word, and mine is mine. Say you couldn't find Ken or myself, we're leaving before sunset, we want to camp in a happier place."

As Steve and Ken rode out of the cave, they were followed by Andrew, Willie and Alf with a pack of fresh meat for a camp yet to be chosen.

Chapter 30

Three months passed and autumn gave way to the long winter days, where Steve and Roy spent their time on Red's property assisting in his work. Mary Bryant was delighted to have Kevin to do the milking, allowing her to do other jobs at that hour in the early morning. Dommy had arrived one day with Roy and Kevin. He had spoken to Red and left the next day although Red wouldn't reveal their conversation.

One morning Red asked Roy to find Steve, because he wanted to talk to them both together over a mug of tea. They duly arrived and waited as he seemed to be gathering his thoughts, as he sipped his tea and then he spoke.

"Your unique Inspector has requested a meeting at a camp five miles north of here. It's a usual camping place, with good water and shade and clear views in all directions. He expects to be passing that place tomorrow morning."

"Do we take meat for him and his escort?" Roy asked.

"Yes, and be ready for him, I'd suggest you leave this afternoon."

"How well do you know him, Red?" Steve asked.

"I've known him a long time, probably as long as you two have known him, but not in the same way," Red laughed and said, "I can't answer any questions about him, other than he is a fine type of man."

The next day at the camp the meat was half cooked and two quart-pots were on the side of a fire, as seven horsemen came riding up the creek, led by the Inspector, John Sefton. As usual Roy and Steve addressed him as Sir, even though they had known him since they were young children.

They looked at him, his black hair had turned grey, he'd managed to keep his slim figure and his eyes still seemed to reach into their souls. They weren't uncomfortable in his presence, just a little wary of his requests.

He gazed at the two young men with a slight smile and mused, "Who would have thought that when I was a young man relaxing in the arms of your adoptive Mother, Susie, she would put forward that audacious plan to me. Now I see it has worked out very well, you were two street urchins, and as I remember, decidedly mischievous, I think you Steve were six years old and Roy was four. Even at four, Roy you knew more about the street life than anyone expected."

"We weren't that bad, Sir," Steve said.

"I was a young man and I always thought you both knew more than you told me, in all the jobs you did for me."

"We saw you frequently with our Mother in various stages of undress," Roy said calmly.

"Relaxing, and she told you to go away because she was busy. I remember that when I was young." He laughed quietly and continued, "I don't think you have changed in the years that I have known you. I can't think of anyone else who can calmly talk about seeing a strange man in bed with their Mother, as you do."

"You were not a strange man, except for the first time we saw you, which wasn't your first time, she told us about you. We had known what it felt like to be hungry, her work put food on the table and you were good for her," Steve replied.

"You employed us as children to do certain undercover jobs for you, we saw some very grim activities on the streets at that time," Roy added.

"That work covered the cost of your education, which was a lot more than boys in your position were ever likely to get at that time," he said, after a moment he continued, "Before you ask, Susie knew that street kids were disappearing on certain nights, that's why she kept you inside, unfortunately for me, when I was visiting her."

Steve and Roy grinned at him, they had been aware he'd taken an interest in their welfare and had given extra money to Susie. It was a secret and never revealed in words. They knew their Mother was fond of him and sometimes asked if they had seen him. There were some questions neither Steve nor Roy could ask him.

"I'm here to congratulate you both on a job well done, this is the second job you've done for me as grown men. In the agreement made with Susie, she requested that you be trained as stockmen, this has now been achieved. Also, in the agreement was for two grants of land. I have talked to Red Bryant and he suggested for you Steve, the block south of his boundary, for you Roy, the block north of "River Oaks," he said. He smiled as he saw the shocked expressions on their faces and continued, "There is a middle block between both of you, it's being reserved for Ken Taylor, who may not be returning to police work, while you two will continue doing special tasks for me."

He stood up and reached into his saddle bag and removed two large envelopes and handed one to each men saying, "These are your Grants and papers, don't lose them."

"Thank you, Sir," they said.

"Susie is a remarkable woman and is determined to do her best for you, she is good at what she does, do you mind?" he said thoughtfully.

"If she's happy, we're happy," Steve replied.

He laughed and spoke in a different soft tone of voice, "Do you know Susie once told me that the police ought to create clubs for the street kids, giving them hope for a better life. A nice idea, but not in my lifetime."

There were the usual farewells, and he mounted his horse and rode back the way he had come with his escort of six troopers. Steve and Roy stood watching him go into the distance,

Steve looked at Roy and asked, "How do two boys from our background get Grants of quality land, as we know these blocks are in this area?'

"We will have to find out," Roy replied.

Chapter 31

"Steve you might want to find out why we've received these grants of land, but you've never enquired too much about John Sefton. We've unquestionably done the jobs he asked us to do since we were children," Roy commented.

"I did once try to ask a question, and he made it plain that we were to obey him."

"Steve, there are too many secrets concerning us, being held by John Sefton. We've slowly built-up knowledge about him."

"Like his escort which isn't a police escort at all, but his security team, five men led by William Knox, his chief of staff."

"Yes, and his office is in Penrith and there's another Inspector Jimmy Straw who is married to Margaret who is John Sefton's sister."

"How do you know about her?" Steve looked surprised and asked.

"She spoke to me once, don't you remember. We were children coming back from doing a job where those nasty old men were in that closed lane. She dropped her fan and you picked it up for her and she gave you a six-penny piece, I think she did it intentionally, don't you remember, you were eight years old at the time."

"I don't remember Roy, why do you remember her?"

"She told me to look after you and I was six years old, I told her I always do, and she gave me a penny."

"I wonder why?"

"Steve, we had just gathered some dangerous information for John Sefton and I think she knew what we had been doing for him."

Steve listened carefully to Roy speaking and wondered, as he often did, about all the detailed information Roy seemed to know about the people surrounding him.

"Roy, we've never spoken about the time we found ourselves in the street, you were four years old and I was six, what do you remember?" he asked.

There was silence, before Roy asked another question, "Have you ever considered that our so called 'Adopted Mother' could actually be our real mother? For reasons best known to herself, she farmed us out to Irenie Cook and Janet Baker. I remember being told that Irenie wasn't my mother. She told me she wasn't my mum, and she fed her own children before I got any food, if there was any left over from the small plates of food she served them. She was jealous of the food I ate. Think Steve, what do you remember?"

"I heard the same words from Janet, she was always complaining that our adopted Mother was making lots of money with all her men friends, while she was struggling to put food on the table. It wasn't a happy place to live. Her husband, if that is what he was in reality as I was never sure the way they use to fight, was fond of hitting me when he was drunk. It was after a really bad bout of getting drunk with Irenie's man that we were pushed out of the door of the only homes we had ever known, into the street."

"I have one other memory of being in the street at that time," Roy said.

"What is it, you've turned pale."

"A man tried to take you away, he said he'd give you a sixpence, he took you by the arm and I screamed at the top of my voice, he let you go and we ran away. Later that morning our adopted Mother found us looking in a garbage bin for any leftover food."

"I have always thought of you as my brother, even when we lived in separate small houses next door to each other. I think it's time we had a talk with Mother," Steve mused.

Roy smiled as he remembered, saying, "I tried talking to her about five years ago, and Mother gave me a lecture about being grateful for having a roof over my head and food on the table and gave me a hug at the end of it."

"We do have a problem now. Mr. Gill has received some information about our Adopted Mother and they're not happy about having a connection with us," Steve informed him.

"The Gill family are going up in the Colonial social world and we would be an embarrassment if we can't produce a satisfactory background to our lives," Roy mused.

"Which means we do really need to speak to John Sefton."

"Do we tell Red Bryant that we're riding to Penrith to see him?" Roy asked

"Yes, in case of a hold-up, someone needs to know our destination."

Red didn't offer any objection to their proposed long ride, but he did offer a warning.

"Be very careful and tread warily in that building you intend to visit; keep wide awake from the moment you enter it until you leave."

"It's police, isn't it?" Roy enquired.

Red replied carefully, "It is and it isn't, tread warily, that's all I can say to you."

*

They enjoyed the long ride and the many places they camped, in particular the camping areas on the Blue Mountains, where there were always interesting people travelling one way or the other. A punt took them across the Nepean River and that was an enjoyable experience. The building they found was in a quiet street on the edge of the town. They rode down the side of it to the stables at the back of the building, where they were met by William Knox who came out of a stable.

"What are you doing here?" he asked In a demanding tone of voice before either Roy or Steve had spoken a word.

Steve's lips tightened before saying, "We've come to speak with Inspector Sefton."

"He isn't available, so you can just leave now."

"No, we're not leaving William, go and ask if Inspector Straw is available to speak to Steve and myself, please?" Roy spoke quietly.

William didn't look happy at being addressed by his Christian name and for a few moments stood undecided, before saying ungraciously, "He'll get rid of you soon enough."

"I wouldn't be too sure about that William," Roy replied, then asked, "Are you usually this sour in the mornings?"

He walked away stiffly, and they followed into the building, along a hallway and up some stairs to an office overlooking the street. A middle-aged man was sitting at a desk covered in papers, he looked up as William announced, "Two visitors Sir, Mr. Baker and Mr. Cook."

He turned on his heel and gave a nasty grin and left the room. The Inspector continued writing before putting down his pen on a rack in front of him, skewed the lid on his ink bottle and sat back in his chair.

"What are you two doing here, you haven't been asked to come here?" he said firmly.

"We've come here to speak with Inspector Sefton, if it is convenient, Sir?" Roy answered politely.

"You can't see him; can I help you?"

"We want to know by what means we were granted two blocks of quality land, Sir?" Steve explained.

A pair of stern eyes glared at them as he said, "How or why has nothing to do with you, I'm busy, please leave now."

"I think we are due an explanation, Inspector." Roy said carefully.

He slammed his hand on his desk saying angrily, "You do, do you. You're nothing but a pair of street kids educated above your station in life, you've no right to question what doesn't concern you, now get out."

Roy showing no emotion at his words, he walked over to the window and looked out on the tree lined street, before turning and facing the angry man in his chair.

"We saved the life of your son, Dommy Straw, did we not?"

"How did you know he was my son?" Inspector Straw asked.

"Not only is he your son, but he was an undercover policeman and had been caught in the valley for a long time," Roy continued.

Inspector Straw sighed and sat back in his chair in a relaxed posture and said, "Alright, you've made your point, I'll tell you what I know about your situation. Since you were young brats Inspector Sefton has given you jobs which had rewards attached to them. These paid for your education. Someone, who will remain nameless, came and demanded you get the reward which the government paid for discovering the counterfeit operation. This paid for the three grants of good land."

"Why would someone make that request?" Steve asked.

"I don't know, it was a total waste of resources to spend it on you."

"Police don't receive rewards for jobs well done?" Roy enquired.

"No, you are correct, but you are not in the regular police. You are in a department of the police, which is normally undercover with special dispensations. I'm busy, if there is nothing else, you can go. When are you leaving to cross the river?"

"We're going to visit our Mother," Steve replied.

"Come and see me on your way home, I may have a job for you."

They left the office and walked back down to the stables, mounted their horses and rode out into the street and out of the town.

Roy stopped at a clump of trees beside the road and said, "Steve we need to talk about something which I've known about for a few years and haven't told you."

"You do have a habit of keeping silent about lots of things, Roy." Steve smiled and said.

"Yes, as long as our lives seem to be in order and there is no visible threat to us, I keep silent. Now we want to marry, and we have a problem. Some years ago, when I was in my twelfth year, I discovered a secret which is closely guarded, and I've never spoken about it."

"I'm listening." Steve said.

"I became curious about the men who were visiting Mother, from what you and I had seen in the streets and other places, these men seemed different, so I peeked through the door which had not been properly closed."

Steve interrupted, "You didn't, did you?'

"Yes, and I saw Mother sitting at a desk writing, fully dressed as usual and the man was speaking in a low voice."

Steve sat quite still on his horse and Roy continued, "Our Mother acts as if she is on the game, but it's only an act, she is engaged in something entirely different connected to John Sefton."

"Roy, I don't understand why you've kept this knowledge secret for all those years since you were a young boy," Steve asked.

"Steve, some secrets are too hard to reveal, a wrong word could cost our Mother her life, I couldn't take that chance, neither of us needed to know anything when I was twelve years old."

Steve expressed his thoughts, "She's tied up in some way with John Sefton and we've seen her in bed with him. It seemed quite ordinary at the time, we never questioned his right to be in her bed, we accepted it as normal."

"We can never reveal this knowledge, Steve."

"Why did you tell me?"

"If anything happens to me, you need to know that our Mother is a good woman, who put food on the table for us kids. Why she did it is not for us to question, that is her secret and we'll continue to give Mother our full support."

"Roy, I want to talk to John Sefton, he is the key to our Mother. We'll continue to play the game on their terms."

Once this decision was made the young men continued their journey to visit their Mother. Roy was aware of the glances from Steve, who wondered how many more secrets his little brother held in his head.

Chapter 32

While Roy and Steve were looking at the growing city, noting the changes since they were last in it, Inspector Jimmy Straw had left the office and walked home to a nicely constructed cottage on the edge of the community. His wife Margaret was on the verandah, where she had been knitting a pullover, using freshly spun merino wool. Like Jimmy, she was tall, neatly attired in a pale blue dress, which suited her cheerful disposition. Jimmy was quite comfortable sitting on the verandah watching her knit. He told her about his day and the visit from Roy Cook and Steve Baker.

"They came to talk to John Sefton and have now gone to see Susie Seaway, the woman who adopted them. What am I going to tell them, when they return and ask to see John?" he said.

"Perhaps some of the truth might help," she suggested, putting her needles down.

"Not without John's permission and he'd never give it. He's your brother, so what do you think I ought to do?"

Margaret smiled, and picking up her needles again, mused, "When I told my Mother I wanted to marry you, she said it was a wise choice because you were intelligent, I've often wondered about that comment she made about you."

Jimmy who had not been listening asked, "What did you say?"

"Nothing dear just thinking aloud."

"It's a bad habit, I never know what you're meaning."

"Probably just as well Jimmy!"

"Well, what do you think?"

She took a big breath and said clearly, "There was the marriage."

"Yes, it was a fake one, I arranged it."

"Not quite dear, the man you chose was unavailable."

"Yes, I know and we got that old drunk to do the job."

Margaret laughed and explained her humour, "He was a real clergyman."

"WHAT did you say?" he shouted.

"You heard me Jimmy, you're sitting beside me. He was a real clergyman who had turned to the bottle. I know some of his ex-parishioners and they'd turn anyone to drink several bottles!"

Jimmy had turned pale at the new thoughts crowding his mind and asked, "Are you telling me that after all these years that it was a real marriage."

"Yes dear, and those 'street urchins' as you call them are your legal nephews."

He was stunned and asked, "Does John know?"

"I shouldn't think so, when I think of all the unsuitable places he has sent those boys when they were children to get information, without a care in the world about what could've happened to them."

"How do you know? You've never seen them."

"Of course, I've seen my nephews and spoken to them."

Jimmy sat still as his wife recounted the fan story and he began to wonder what else she was keeping from him, as she spoke briskly in that no argument tone of voice, which she sometimes used in the mornings.

"I was pleased to hear Susie insisted upon her sons getting the grants of land acquired with the reward money for locating the counterfeit operations."

"How do you know about this secret information?"

"Susie Sefton is a friend of mine Jimmy," adding, "So how much of the truth are you going to tell John Sefton's sons?"

"Margaret you are not meant to know her; this is very awkward."

"Leave my friend Susie to the mercy of you men, no Jimmy. So, what will you tell the boys who are your nephews?'

Jimmy looked horrified and replied "I will not see them at all. William Knox will say he is unavailable which is the truth."

"One day Jimmy they will have to be told the truth.'

"That is for John to do, not me."

They talked about the other events in their day.

Chapter 33

The next morning Jimmy Straw walked to his office deep in thought of what his wife had told him. Instead of going into the building he walked to the horse yard to find William Knox talking to a couple of men who had never treated him with the respect he felt was due, they had bypassed him and gone to John Sefton. Their attitude was about to change, he thought to himself, not long now before a death notice would appear in the newspaper. William Knox he'd sack at the first opportunity or better still he'd have an accident, because he knew too much about the current problem.

"Saddle the grey mare for me please," he asked one of the men.

"Where are you going Inspector?" Knox stood up and asked.

"Out for a few hours, Knox."

Jimmy could see that Knox hated being addressed by his surname, though it was customary to address employees in this way. He thanked the man for saddling his horse and rode out of the yard. He didn't want Knox to know the direction he was intending to ride on leaving the village, so took a couple of detours before riding eastwards. There were small communities a few miles apart, with fruit trees, vegetable gardens and stock paddocks. At one village he rode up to a well-constructed house, entering by a side gate, he rode around to the back of the dwelling to the stables, dismounting and tying his horse up to a hitching rail. Jimmy turned to see a man walk out of the back door. He was out of his uniform and in civilian clothes, well dressed and of a pale complexion and a dark well-trimmed beard.

"What are you doing here at this time of the day, Jimmy?" he asked.

"I have some information which is disturbing and felt it needed to be reported to you as soon as possible, Frank."

"Come inside, we can't talk out here."

Frank took him into the kitchen which was a separate building at the back of the house. They had a habit of burning down and were kept at a distance from the more valuable rooms. Now seated in front of an open fire, holding mugs of tea, Frank asked, "What is it, Jimmy?"

"I learnt from my wife yesterday that John Sefton legally married Susie Seaway, it wasn't a fake wedding as we'd arranged. Margaret swapped the drunk ordinary man for a drunk Minster. It is legal. Furthermore, she gave birth to his two sons, Steve and Roy."

Frank laughed before enquiring, "Does Sefton know any of this information?"

"Margaret says no, he has been kept in the dark for some reason."

Frank laughed again and explained, "Thank you Jimmy for telling me, it is too delicious for words. This new information won't alter our plans at all, after Sefton is dead, Susie will follow and her sons."

"What do you mean, that Susie has to die?"

"Don't be dumb Jimmy, you set the whole business in motion, of course they will have to die and some others too, there can be no witnesses.'

"You know I didn't set the whole nightmare in motion," Jimmy spluttered.

"I know but you're the front man, Jimmy!"

"At that time I didn't know the boys were my nephews."

"No matter, don't get squeamish now Jimmy, it's too late for that."

"What do you mean Frank?"

"The order has gone out for Sefton's execution, and another will go out for his wife."

"I don't like it Frank, it was never meant to include his family," Jimmy said, turning pale.

"Too late Jimmy, Sefton was close to making a discovery of our activities and we're not prepared to lose all that lovely money."

Jimmy made one last appeal for mercy for the family.

"We're police."

"We have the power to do what we want to do, and Jimmy we are going to keep the good times going for as long as we can keep control," Frank laughed and replied, adding, "Jimmy you're up to your neck in this business, you've betrayed your brother-in-law for years, so buck up and take your share of the spoils. As we've told you before, you can have John's position."

Jimmy looked hard into Frank's eyes, they were as cold and hard as any frost in winter.

"Oh, Margaret, what have I done," he whispered as he rode away from the house.

He remembered Frank's words 'No witnesses', this now included Margaret.

He knew he'd never get John's position; he'd be fortunate to keep his own life.

Chapter 34

Steve and Roy rode to the edge of the city and as usual left their horses at the Waterloo Hotel stables which was owned by their friend Luke White. Word soon reached him that two old friends were in his stables, and he came out the back door to greet them.

"Come in and have a pint, I haven't seen either of you for such a long time," he said cheerfully.

Steve slapped him on the back saying, "It's good to see you again Luke, how is Charlotte and the little ones?"

"Cut it out Steve, we've only got two children!"

"No doubt more are on the way!"

"We want a large family, but not just yet."

"That means stopping your enjoyment and I can't see that happening any time soon!" Roy laughed and said.

Luke laughed and said quietly, "It's really good to see you both, come inside where we can talk without anyone hearing our conversation. He took them inside to a small sitting room behind the public drinking area, a safe place to talk.

"With all the talking in the drinking area, no one could hear a word spoken in here," Roy commented.

"I made it for that reason, certain visitors I have at times can't be overheard, like yourselves. Do I assume you are on your way to visit your Mother?" Luke said.

"Yes, have you heard anything that we should know about before we go to see her?" Roy replied.

Luke walked to the doorway and looked out of it, seeing no one, he spoke quietly, "Be careful, this has become dangerous territory, no one is safe if there is the slightest suspicion of having worked for John Sefton."

"Do you know what is going on with certain police?" Steve asked.

"No, I don't. I keep well out of it. All his old team have gone to ground if possible or gone bush,"

Both Steve and Roy were deeply disturbed at this new information and Steve asked gently, "Mother?"

"I don't know," he said quietly, "Other than she is close to John Sefton, this has always been so since she was a young girl and he was a young man." Luke suddenly smiled and continued, "If you can imagine Inspector being that young!"

Steve smiled and said, "We can, we've known him since we were children Luke, and have become accustomed to him being in our lives."

"I suppose that accounts for all the things he has done for you and Roy."

"How much is known about John Sefton's relationship with us?" Steve asked.

"You mean the reward money?"

"Yes, and other events."

Luke took a long drink from his mug, as if he was gathering his thoughts together to answer the question.

"Steve we were a tightly bound group, and we weren't blind to the fact that John Sefton favoured you and Roy. We have our own suspicions, as to why this is. It's never bothered us, but there's another group of police who have been playing the system for years. They are now getting the upper hand; Sefton was close to having them arrested."

"For this to happen, he must have been betrayed, any ideas?" Roy asked.

"The word is his brother-in- law," Luke replied in a whisper.

"Makes sense, he isn't a strong man, nor is he intelligent enough or ruthless enough to operate this present situation," Steve added.

"I'd say that piece of information was leaked to you for a purpose. It hides the real man operating behind Jimmy Straw," Roy commented.

Luke finished his ale and said, "Give my best wishes to your Mother."

Steve taking the hint replied, "Our best wishes to Charlotte too, Luke."

As they left the building Luke said, "Your horses are safe here, the chances are good that when you return, you'll be under observation. Please don't show in any way you know me."

Impulsively he gave Steve and Roy a big hug and each man understood, without words being spoken. Luke opened the side door, looked out and saw the street was empty, Steve and Roy went out and down the roadway.

They enjoyed their brisk walk, looking at all the changes which had occurred since they'd roamed this area a few years ago. By late afternoon they arrived in the street where their Mother had her Tea Rooms. They found it closed up, picking up their pace, they found their way to her rented rooms, to be told rudely, "She's moved."

"Where to?" Roy asked.

"She's got that tiny cottage in between the two big warehouses in Duck Street, you know it boy?"

"Yes, we know it."

It was indeed a tiny brick cottage, of four equally tiny rooms, not enough as one of her friends told her to 'swing a cat' as the saying goes, but it was home. They found it easily enough because it had a past well known to Steve and Roy. Smiling at each other they knocked on the front door. For a moment or two they didn't recognise the middle-aged woman who opened the door a crack and peered out.

She saw her lovely sons and said briskly, "Come in, don't stand there like dummies, give me a kiss"

Not only a kiss, but big hugs as well, after she'd closed the front door. She saw Steve's expression and asked, "What are you thinking?"

"Mother, you are still a beautiful woman."

She beamed and hugged him and then Roy saying, "You don't know how good it is to see you both again."

Roy noticed a new type of desperation in the way she went about doing work in her cottage.

"Mother we need to talk," he said at the end of their lunch the next day.

She looked up from her plate and replied, "There may not be time Roy."

"Mother, we've learnt that John Sefton was betrayed by Jimmy Straw, who is behind him we don't know yet. Our deep concern is for you now," Steve spoke quietly.

The surprise on her face was total and she replied in almost a whisper, "You know?"

"Not a lot, Mother, but we have always known that you have acted being on the game, when you were actually gathering information for John Sefton." Roy continued.

"How did you know that Roy?"

"When I was twelve, you forgot to close the door properly and I peeked!"

"You kept my secret all those years, did you know Steve?" she laughed and said.

"No Mother, Roy has just told me."

"What else do you know Steve?" she asked.

He looked straight at her and said, "We know you're our real Mother."

"How long have you known it?"

"From the moment you found us looking for scraps of food in the garbage bins. You thought your heart would burst in shock. You had already discovered we'd been turned out into the street by the two women you'd paid to feed us. Instead they'd used the money to feed their own children, only giving us the leftovers, including their worn-out clothes," Roy answered.

"Have you ever wondered why I put you with those two women?" she asked.

"We think you had a good reason at the time. It's over and done with now," Roy replied.

"Is John Sefton our father?" Steve asked.

"How do you both feel about him?" she asked, sidestepping the question.

"We are fond of him in our way."

"Yes, he is your father," she smiled.

She hugged her sons tightly before explaining about her earlier world. They heard about the fake marriage and that he didn't know he was legally married to her. Her sons laughed and she added, "He doesn't know you are his sons."

"Does this knowledge change anything for you Mother?" Steve asked.

"NO! It's important to maintain I'm on the game until we can talk to John in safety," then adding, "I know about Anne Roy, let it play out and see what happens, there are lives at risk."

"I understand Mother," Roy smiled.

They left the next morning after a heartwarming visit, the best time in years with the knowledge of their own realities.

"I peeked into her room before leaving, she had all her belongings packed up, she never let on in any way, but I think Mother is going into hiding," Roy said quietly to Steve, after collecting their horses.

"What do we do Roy?"

"We go back to the Office and ask to see John Sefton of course. This way they will think we are ignorant of what is building up as a major operation of the good police."

They smiled at each other and rode towards Penrith.

Chapter 35

Jimmy Straw rode home deeply disturbed for the welfare of his wife Margaret, unthinkingly he had just betrayed her to a dangerous man. It had not occurred to him to consider what Frank might do to her if he felt she had other knowledge of the Sefton family. Only one thought was in his mind, she had to leave as soon as it could be arranged and go to her cousin, who had a farm just outside the community of Last Stop. His main worry was how to tell her. Margaret would have to leave secretly as soon as possible.

Jimmy unsaddled the grey mare in his own stables, he'd take it back to the police yard later. He did hope none of his men saw his detour to his own house as it would only create questions. He found Margaret on the front verandah spinning wool, a job she loved doing, when he had enquired, she had replied, "Time to think Jimmy, time to think."

She was surprised to see him here at this time of the day, he came and sat down near her, she took one look at his face and made a guess.

"You've been and told Frank, haven't you Jimmy?"

"How do you know?'

"You talk in your sleep."

"How long have I talked in my sleep?"

"Since I married you, Jimmy."

"So you know?"

"Yes Jimmy."

"Margaret, I'm sorry. John always got the best of everything, and I felt it was my turn. If he could just disappear! Then he gave those three men that land, it wasn't just the reward money, he put his own money into it to make up the difference, money we could have had for a better life."

"Jimmy, I wouldn't have let you touch my brother's money. We have had a good life but now you have sided with Frank, and it's all about to come crumbling down on our heads."

"I want you to leave secretly and take a dray of your favourite things from this house, you will not be able to return any time soon." he said firmly.

Margaret smiled sadly and said, "I've already sent two drays to my cousin, they left in the night, you may have noticed gaps in the furniture?'

"I've been too worried to notice anything. When can you leave Margaret?" he asked.

"Are you coming with me Jimmy?'

"No, I can't leave the Office just yet, Steve Baker and Roy Cook are coming to see me on their way back from visiting their Mother and want to talk to me, they'll be asking to see John."

"What will happen?"

"William Knox will get rid of them for me."

"How Jimmy?"

"Oh! You needn't worry, he won't hurt them, yet."

Margaret stood up and folded up a ball of wool and put the remainder of the merino fleece in a bag. She turned and looked down at her husband and spoke sadly, "Jimmy we had a good life together, until you became greedy and linked yourself to Frank."

"Frank was a good policeman, I know you never liked him, you just don't know him," Jimmy said.

Surprise flashed across her face as she said, "You do know who Frank is don't you Jimmy?"

"What are you talking about, he's a policeman."

"Yes, Frank is unfortunately a policeman," adding, "He is believed to be connected to the man who died in the children's pit of meat ants. Now you know why he wants Steve Baker and Roy Cook to be killed."

Jimmy sat still in his chair, shocked into silence and gradually voiced in whispers, "NO..no..no."

"Yes, Susie warned me to flee while I can do so."

"How long have you known?"

"Long enough to get packing Jimmy."

"I'm in deep trouble," he sat still and said.

"More than that Jimmy, you have just told the most lethal man in the city, that you are the blood uncle of his most hated man, Steve Baker. How could you have been so thoughtless."

He sat as all colour drained from his face and asked in a whisper, "When are you leaving Margaret?"

"Tonight, if I can, my last dray will go across on the punt in the late afternoon and I will cross in the early morning."

"You are taking this parting very calmly, I must say"

"My tears have all been shed, I've watched you betray my brother and nephews. If you can leave, and I hope you will be able to, make for Last Stop. I'll be waiting."

*

A few days later Roy and Steve rode into the stable yard and were most surprised to see Alex Pitt and Charley exit the stables and called out to them.

"Alex, Charley."

They walked across the yard as Roy and Steve dismounted.

"You both work for John Sefton too?" Roy asked.

"Yes, we've worked for him for some time and you?"

"Since we were children," Steve replied.

At that moment William Knox came out of the stables and said to Steve, "Get back on your horses, you can't speak to Inspector Straw, he's out of his office and Inspector John Sefton isn't here now."

When will it be convenient to speak to John Sefton?" Steve asked.

"I don't know, he's missing," he replied, smiling unpleasantly.

ACKNOWLEDGEMENTS

This is my second year of learning how to use a computer. The pages still vanish but not as often as they did when I was writing *The Frontier*.

I'm grateful for the efforts of Sam Everingham who took the time to write a letter of improvements I have used to improve the script. This book is the result of his suggestions of 'keeping secrets'!

I'm still using one finger to type but my spelling has improved. The script is written in longhand, rewritten and eventually typed. I thank Wendy Morrow for her work in correcting sentences and other errors.

I also thank Kayla Arkinstall and Huw Moore for coming to my house to put my work on USB drives.

I wish to thank Ted Lewis for the use of one of his paintings for the cover.

This is the second book in a trilogy.